VOLUME 2 OF THE claire goodnite SERIES

tuck me in + tight

jennifer rebecca

Tuck Me In Tight

Cover Design by:
Alyssa Garcia
www.uplifting-designs.com

Editing by:
Stephanie Atienza
www.uplifting-designs.com
ISBN: 978-1-7320747-2-9

For more information about Jennifer Rebecca or her books, visit:
www.JenniferRebeccaAuthor.com

in loving memory . . .

Charlotte Jameson Atienza

November 14, 2017—November 17, 2017
For three days we held and angel in our arms and those
were three of the best days of our lives. On her third day
on earth, she went to sleep and never woke up. Charlotte
was truly too beautiful for earth and born with a purpose far
greater than we will ever comprehend.

While we will never truly understand the how or the
why of infant loss our hearts go out to the families who have
walked the same path. We miss her every day and know that
we will hold her in our arms again one day.

As it always is with loss so deep, one day the dark sky
will break into a beautiful dawn until then . . .

If our story has moved you please consider making a
donation in honor of Charlotte to one of the following orga-
nizations so that we may one day see an end to infant death.

The March of Dimes (marchofdimes.org)
The American SIDS Institute (sids.org)

"Like a comet pulled from orbit
As it passes a sun
Like a stream that meets a boulder
Halfway through the wood
Who can say if I've been changed for the better?
Because I knew you
I have been changed for good . . ."
-*For Good* (Idina Menzel and Kristin Chenoweth)

dedication

To the last boy who ever broke my heart,
It hurt and at the time, I didn't know that the hurt
would ever stop, but it was a blessing because it freed
my heart to find Sean and he is my everything. He has
given me a life of beauty. Our children are my world
and I find a reason to smile and laugh every day. You
were right to walk away when you did. Thank you.
Also, thank you for not becoming a serial killer.

tuck
me in
+ tight

prologue

THIS IS HOW MY heart breaks
What. The. Fuck.

I had sat down at my desk and opened a manila envelope that was left on top of my stack of mail. It had seemed harmless enough.

But it wasn't.

I blink my eyes over and over trying to make my brain process what it's seeing—but I can't. I can't unsee the images in the stack of pictures in my hand. Giant glossy eight by tens from different angles so there is absolutely no doubt that my heart is breaking.

And it is broken. It's not just broken, it's *shattered*.

"It's not what it looks like," I hear from behind me as he looks over my shoulder and I have to grit my teeth to keep from screaming.

I shuffle the pictures sliding the top one to the back of the stack so that I can see the next one. This one is zoomed in. His head is tipped back and his face is distorted with both lust and passion as she straddles his lap. Her hands hold his to her breasts and I can see the play of tendons flexing through them as he grips them tight. It was only two nights ago that his hands were on my own breasts in much the same way as I rode his cock on the sofa.

"Claire, did you hear me?" he asks but I shuffle the stack again.

In this picture, he has his arms wrapped around her back and he's pulling her close, her breasts mashed up against his strong chest. Her hands with long, red painted talons press in on either side of his face and as they kiss hungrily, their mouths open as their tongues tangle.

"Goddamnit, Claire! Did you hear me?" My spine turns to steel.

"I did. I'm just choosing to ignore you," I respond coolly.

"Don't do this, baby," he pleads.

"I'm not the one who did anything," I snap.

"I can explain." But I'm not interested in listening to him plead a case when he is more than guilty.

"I'm going to need you to leave, Wes."

"No."

"This changes everything," I say so softly even I struggle to hear the words that are coming out of my mouth.

"This changes nothing! Fuck that, Claire," he yells. "You want to run away. You have *always* wanted to run away. And here is your fucking reason to served up on a goddamn silver platter." Everyone around us in the bullpen is doing everything they can to make it appear that they are not listening, not studying the tragic demise of Claire and Wes with rapt attention. But we all know that they are.

"No," I shout back as I throw the stack of glossy betrayal down on top of my desk. I push my rolly chair back and stand. It slams into the desk behind mine. "You do not get to come in here, where I work, and tell me that I am to blame for your bullshit."

"Okay," he says quickly as he holds his hands up in surrender. "You're right. I'm sorry. I can see you need time."

"I need a lot of things. One of them is definitely distance."

"I don't know if I can give you that. I can't lose you, baby." His words burn hot behind my eyes and the last thing I want is for the guys in the bullpen to see me cry.

"You should have thought about that before you fooled around with that stripper."

"Claire—" he starts but I don't let him finish.

"You need to go now," I say softly.

I stand with my feet apart, my hands on my hips, and my head bowed as if I'm waiting for a blow. But I see him clearly even if only in my peripheral. He looks at me and opens his mouth as if he's going to try to explain again. Something in my stance must have told him it was a losing battle because he snaps his mouth closed before moving towards the exit.

Wes pauses just before opening the door to turn and look back at me, I see him in my peripheral, but I'm looking at his lies and deceit spread across my desk for all to see. He pulls open the door and slams it on his way out. I'm Detective Claire Goodnite and this is how my heart breaks.

chapter 1

bad girl

48 hours earlier . . .

"Fuck," HE GROANS AS I unzip his jeans and reach in, pulling out his hard cock.

It doesn't take much to have Wes hard and wanting—needing me and I love it. I had just finished dressing for the evening as he had let himself into my apartment. Wes had said that he wanted to see me before he went off to Jones's bachelor party and I went to dinner with Emma and Anna.

I'm wearing a tight black dress and matching four-inch heels. Anna wanted to check out some new swanky place in the city and despite spending her days being elbows deep in dead people, Emma can really turn herself out. She loves a good stiletto and I would hate to be the ugly friend in the group.

I'm standing over my bathroom counter slicking my lips a deep, sexy pink. I feel him standing there, my body always knows when Wes is near and it always has in one way or another. Deep in my heart I wonder if Wes and I were always meant to be.

I feel myself cracking, caving in, to love him. I fought it so hard but as it turns out, I never had a choice in the matter.

I cap the pink color and set it down just as he clears his throat. Then uncap the clear gloss that goes on top. I turn my head to look at him and the mood in the room goes electric. His gaze scorches my face as he looks me over. My face, my mouth, down to my breasts where they press up and out of the top of my dress, down my waist and hips to where the hem falls just shy of showing anything important and down, down my legs, before snapping back up to meet my eyes. By the sizeable bulge in jeans—he likes what he sees.

I smirk as I turn back to the mirror and slick my lips with the gloss. A feral growl rips from deep within his chest as he grips my hips in his hands and pulls me into him, his hard length cradled between my thighs as I lean over the counter. I drop my gloss to the vanity top.

Wes slides one palm down my belly and then down, down, down to press against my sex over my dress. He presses the fingertips of his other hand to my jaw to turn my head before crushing his mouth to mine in a hungry kiss.

When he pulls back I'm out of breath and wet.

"You're so fucking sexy," he pants. "Tonight, all I'll be thinking about is what might be underneath this dress and what those shiny pink lips look like wrapped around my cock."

"Then maybe you should find out." My voice is husky with my arousal.

"First things first," he says as his hand at the apex of my thighs slides a little lower. He hooks his fingers under the hem of my skirt and inches it higher and higher as he nibbles at the spot behind my ear that does things to me.

I open my eyes and look in the mirror. I gasp at what I see. The couple in front of me burns in the heat of passion. Her purple eyes are bright with excitement. Her skirt is rucked up around her waist exposing a tiny, lace thong with pencil thin strings.

The man stands not only behind her, but all around her—lost to her and his need. He not only worships her body as he kisses and caresses but possesses it as well. I'm lost in the vision of Wes and me. His dark smoky eyes open and meet my bright ones in the mirror making me burn for him from the inside out.

"So, you want to watch?" he asks.

I bite my lip and just nod. I'm unable to find the words to tell him what I want, what I need, but then again, Wes always knows before I do. He hooks his fingers in my panties and slides them to the side, sliding his fingers through my opening but not pressing deep enough.

"My bad girl is so wet for me."

"Yes," I pant as he swirls his index finger around my clit. I want to buck my hips to ride his fingers, but Wes has me pressed between his hard body and the counter. I'm unable to move anywhere.

"I love it when you burn for me," he says as he slips his other hand down the front of my dress and pinches my nipple—hard—as he applies pressure to my clit.

I gasp. "Wes—"

"I know, baby," he nips at my ear overloading my senses. "Just a little bit more."

Wes pushes two fingers into my pussy and hits just the spot as his thumb takes over circling my clit. I pant as my fingers lose their grip on the counter and I reach for Wes to keep me grounded. I grip one of his forearms in each hand—up at my breast and down at my center—as he pushes me closer and closer to the edge of bliss.

I tip my head back against his chest and moan as my nails score his tanned skin.

"I've got you, baby. Just. Let. Go," he says as he rolls my nipple between his thumb and index finger as his other hand pumps hard and fast. His thumb flicks my clit faster and faster. "Let go," he commands as he pinches my nipple and I do with my head thrown back on his shoulder as I scream his name.

Wes lightly kisses my neck while his fingers slowly slip in and out of my heat until I can't take it anymore. My heart rate slows and my breathing is less choppy. I open my eyes and meet his in the mirror.

"You're the sexiest woman on the planet, Claire," he says and I can feel his hard length press into my ass as he rocks his hips just a bit. "What are you doing to me?" I smirk.

"Well, I could tell you what I'm about to do to you … but I'd rather show you," I reply to him as I turn in his arms.

Wes crushes his mouth to mine in more than a kiss, it's a meeting of lips and teeth and tongues. It's hard and hot. I push his worn leather jacket from his shoulders and let it fall to the bathroom floor. His belt buckle clanks as I unhook it and pull his zipper down before pushing him backwards so that his shoulders collide with the wall.

"Fuck," he groans as I reach in and pull out his hard cock.

I push his jeans and boxer briefs down his hips together so that his hard length can spring free before dropping to my knees in front of him, my skirt still hiked up over my hips. Wes watches me on my knees before him like a hungry predator. His eyes lock to mine as he licks the fingers that were just in my most secret places. It renews my lust and I have to squeeze my thighs together on an aftershock of my own.

"I want that pink smeared on my dick while I'm at the club. I want your mark on my body," he commands but I have a surprise for him as I wrap my fist around him and pump his cock once … twice before licking the tip.

I let my eyes meet his with the tip of his cock just brushing my stained lips. "It's the kind that doesn't smear."

"Oh fuck. That's hot."

"I know," I say before taking the tip into my mouth and swirling it around.

Wes groans deep and loud before tangling his fingers in my curls and pulling just to the point that it stings. He rocks his hips and I let his cock slide in and out of my mouth, deeper and deeper. I pump his base in my fist as he pumps in and out of my mouth.

"So good, baby. Suck me harder." And I do. I know he's close because his movements are becoming a little frantic. "Fuck, fuck, fuck. Jesus Christ it's so good."

I squeeze him tighter in my fist and move my hand faster and faster. He pulls at my hair with his hands and groans.

"Yes, oh fuck yes. Baby, I'm going to come." Above all else, I love that I am the only one that takes him there. "Claire," he shouts as his whole body tightens and he pours himself into my mouth. I swallow every last drop.

Wes pulls me to my feet and wraps his arms around me tight, crushing his mouth to mine. His tongue licks in and I'm lost to his kiss. When he pulls back, there's an emotion playing behind his eyes but I'm not ready to put a name to it.

"What?" I ask.

"That mouth," he growls. "Will be the death of me."

I shrug. "I just felt compelled to remind you of what you're leaving behind while you're in that strip club."

"Do you not want me to go?" he asks suddenly concerned.

"No, not at all," I smile. "I'm going out to the city with Emma and Anna."

"Or we could both not go out," he growls. "And I could fuck you on the bathmat."

"As tempting as that is," I say patting his chest while he groans at my rebuff. "We're going out."

"Not if we have a better offer," he says as he backs me up into the counter and hikes one leg around his waist. His still hard cock rubs against my pussy and I whimper at the connection. "You're still wet for me. Still so hot for me. I could make you feel better, baby. . . End that suffering," he says as his cock glides through my wetness.

I arch my back and rock my hips against his hard length getting closer and closer to the knife's edge of bliss but I know that if I come on his cock, Wes will fuck me on the bath mat just like he promised. While a night of carnal pursuits with Wes is amazing, we need to get out and if all that starts we never will. So I kiss him one more time before gently pushing against his chest. He groans again when he realizes I'm telling him no.

"Just think," I tell him. "In a few hours we can drunk fuck. It will be fun."

"With you, it always is, baby."

We straighten our clothes and there is not one damn thing I can do about the sex hair, but it's kind of hot so I go with it. Wes just laughs and swats my ass as we walk out the door to meet our friends. He's going to drop me off with Anna before heading across town to meet the guys at the club.

I look up at his handsome face and smile. We've never been so close. Wes has burrowed so deep into my life and my heart. If only I had known that in a few short hours that foundation would be rocked—that everything would change. Maybe I would have stayed home after all. Then again, *maybe not*.

chapter 2

nothing bad

*S*HE'S MINE.

I have to have her. I need the bad girl. I watched as she danced for a man that shouldn't want her. I watched as she rubbed her body all over his with lust in her eyes. She wants him too. And the hard-on in my pants shows how much I want her. It's a conundrum of sorts.

When she kisses him, thrusting her pink tongue into his mouth I have to look away and shift my body to ease the burn in my balls.

She finishes her dance and takes the bills he offers her but nothing more. His loss is my gain. She stands from his lap and walks through the club. I follow her down the hall. My companions don't miss me, they think I'm making a phone call out front.

"Hey," she says jumping when I startle her. "I didn't see you there."

"My apologies, I didn't mean to frighten you."

"You didn't," she's quick to add.

"You smoke?" I ask holding up a pack that I always carry with me for just this purpose.

"Now you're speaking my language," she laughs as she pushes through the exit door at the end of the hallway. "Join me?"

"Of course."

I tap a cigarette out of the pack and point it at her, my fingers never touching the actual cigarette. She doesn't seem to notice as she only has eyes for the slim white stick and the lighter in my other hand. She turns away from me to light it, not wanting to be rude and blow smoke in my face. This is my opportunity and it's perfect, just like I planned.

She never noticed me slipping on a pair of latex gloves. Her lack of cognizance will be her downfall.

She doesn't even make a noise when the needle slips into her neck. Her body goes rigid as she falls, but her eyes are wide. She sees everything.

I stamp out her cigarette on the asphalt under my boot and drag her behind the dumpster. We don't have much time, something I will lament later, hopefully much later.

I lay her down on the ground behind the dumpster and strip off her G-string. That's it, that's all there is. She didn't even bother to cover up before she came out here with me to smoke.

Her eyes flash with her unspoken why.

"I wish I could tell you," I whisper to her as I straddle her hips, my erection pressing into her mound through my pants. "I won't apologize to you though, I need this more than you could ever understand."

My belt buckle clanks in the silence as I undo my

pants. I slip a condom down my hard length and I wrap my hands around her slim neck. Her lovely purple eyes go wide.

"So lovely," I say as I poise my tip at her entrance. I don't bother to spread her legs, she'll be tighter this way. I apply the perfect amount of pressure as I slide in. I revel in the blood vessels popping in her eyes as I steal the breath from her lungs. "Yes, absolutely lovely."

"Stop!" I laugh clutching my belly. There's a real fear that my Macallan 18 is about to come out my nose. That would really burn.

"I'm serious!" Emma shouts just a little drunk on her martini. "You would have grabbed your panties and left too."

"I think that seems a little cruel," Anna shares, obviously feeling bad for the man with the tiny dick.

"I'm just saying, 'ain't nobody got time for that!'"

"I mean I know it's not eight inches, but … it can't be that small," Anna rallies.

"Oh, it was. It was smaller than my thumb." Emma laments.

"So, you just left?" I ask.

"Of course. I stood up, grabbed my panties, said, 'Don't call me,' and left," she answers.

"Have you heard from him?" Anna asks obviously feeling bad for the poor guy.

"Ugh, don't get me started."

"No, let's." I clap my hands with glee like a circus monkey. Emma's dating woes are some of my most favorite bedtime stories.

"Asshole," she coughs.

"Please," I beg holding my hands up in prayer fashion.

"Ugh. Okay, fine, but don't say I didn't warn you," she clarifies before continuing her dating tale of woe. "Not only has he spent all week calling and leaving me voicemail messages about how much he loves me and misses me..."

"Homeboy loves you?" I ask, cutting her off.

"Apparently," Emma drolls.

"How long did you guys go out?" Anna asks.

"One."

"One month? One Week? One Year?" I ask. "Help us out here, Em."

"One. Fucking. Date. He's a God damned stage five clinger."

"That's not very nice talk for a doctor," I remind her laughing.

"Fuck off," she laughs as she flips me the bird.

"So not only is he a clinger… but what?" I ask.

"His *girlfriend* sent me a Facebook message telling me to back off her man."

"No!" Anna and I both say at the same time.

"Tiny dick has a regular girlfriend?" I ask.

"Oh yeah, the prick—pun intended."

"Shut up," Anna chokes out through her laughter.

"Go ahead, yuck it up you little shits," she sighs as she takes another big sip of her martini. "Is it so much to ask for eight inches of hard cock on a built alpha guy with a good job that worships me?"

"Yes!" Anna and I both say simultaneously.

"You shut your damn mouth. She points a drunken finger at me and closes one eye to better focus on me.

"Clearly, she's ingested more gin than steak," Anna whispers to me.

"I heard that!" Emma snaps. "But I was talking to you."

"Me? What did I do?"

"You have eight inches of hard cock on an alpha god waiting for you."

"He's not perfect," I tell her. "And neither am I."

"Say that to my face when you don't have sex hair," she laughs.

"I do not!" I shout as I comb my hair with my fingers.

"You totally do," Anna laughs.

"Ugh fine. So, Wes is pretty great. So, what?"

"Nothing bad," Emma says. "It's just proof that it's out there and we shouldn't settle for less."

"Like little dicks?" Anna asks.

"Exactly," Emma answers. "We won't settle for little dicks. The real deal is out there."

I open my mouth to shoot her a sassy reply about all of the tiny, and not so tiny, dicks she has encountered in her search to find the perfect cock when my phone rings. It's Liam's ring. I sigh.

"What's wrong?" Anna asks me.

"Nothing. That's Liam's ring. Wes must be super drunk and needing a ride home."

I pull my phone from my purse. I missed the call but it immediately starts ringing again. "Hello?" I answer.

"Claire, it's Lee. I need you. There's been a homi-cide."

chapter 3

step on it

"*SO, WHAT HAPPENED WAS...*"

"Let me stop you right there," I say as I clench my fists in an effort not to scream. I am so freaking mad right now.

There I was, having a great girls' night out with Emma and Anna, when my phone rang. Never before in my life have I been so scared as when I answered the phone. I will never forget the sound of my brother, Liam, telling me that he needed my help.

Emma, Anna, and I threw down copious amounts of cash to get us out of the swanky NYC restaurant we had been dining in while Lee and Wes were at a bachelor party. Anna threw her scotch back like a boss and we headed out in the night air. We all knew that it would take us awhile to get back to New Jersey and time was of the essence.

We grabbed our purses and wraps and beat feet out the door. Our feet—in ridiculous heels by the way—ate up the sidewalk as we made our way to the coffee cart that sits on a corner about a block away from *Filet de Boeuf*, the fancy assed restaurant that Anna insisted we splurge on.

After dropping five dollars on three black coffees, Emma stepped her long ass legs just off the curb, her skirt hiking up just enough as she raised one hand over head. The fingers of her other hand were in her mouth letting out a whistle that would make any New York baseball fan proud.

A yellow cab comes screeching to a halt in front of us—thank God not over us— and Anna pulls the front passenger door open and drops in offering the cabbie her dazzling smile. Her real mission is to distract him so that Emma and I can haul ass into the back seat and shut the door behind us.

"Where to, gorgeous?" he asks.

"George Washington Township, New Jersey." She smiles brightly at him knowing full well what he's about to say in his heavily accented voice. We all do. Emma and I smirk at eat other in the back seat.

"No! No New Jersey! Get out of my cab."

"We can't do that," Anna pouts.

"Why not?" he shouts. "You get out now or I call cops."

"Lucky for you, we are cops." I smile at him as Emma and I hold up our various badges.

"Cop!" he yells as he pulls on his thinning hair. I hope he doesn't pull too hard, he doesn't have much left to lose. "Freaking cops."

"Yes, Sir. And could you please step on it."

"Ugh," he lets out a strangled sound before pulling away from the curb at breakneck speed. When he enters the highway breaking the land speed record, I think I've found my soulmate. I see him taking the first exit for George Washington Township when he shouts, "Where to, crazy lady cops?"

"Technically, I'm the Medical Examiner," Emma says after clearing her throat.

"And I'm the department shrink," Anna admits through her laughter on a delicate shoulder shrug.

"You tricked me!" he wails. "You're not even real cops!"

"Well, I am a real cop," I sigh at my two best friends and their ridiculousness. "And we need to go to the Pink Kitty Lounge."

"That place is disgusting!" He spits. "Why do you want to go there? Are you whores?"

"No!" we all shout at the same time.

"Only girls there are tricks and dancers," he says adamantly.

"We have a case there," I explain.

"That's not much better. You should be home with your babies," he says with all seriousness.

"He must be in the same bridge group as my mother," Emma growls. I just throw my head back and laugh. We all get the same crap from our families *When are you going to meet a nice man? When are you going to get married? When are you going to have babies?* Too bad we're all busy fighting crime and taking down the bad guys. But that's alright by us. We wouldn't have it any other way.

Before I know it, we're pulling into the front lot of the Pink Kitty Lounge. Police cars are everywhere, the sirens off but the blue and red lights swirling on top. The cab comes to a stop and we all pile out of the yellow car as I hand a credit card to the cabbie—who gives me the side eye for not having two hundred and seventy-eight dollars and fifty-two cents in cash. How dare I?

I roll my eyes as he hands back my card and I slip it into my little clutch. I will be filing an expense report in the morning, thank you very much!

"Where have you been?" Liam yells as he comes into my line of sight.

"Well, hello to you too, brother dearest." I bow. Man, I was hoping he wasn't going to be a pompous windbag but I guess I spoke too soon.

"This is serious, Claire," he says as he grabs my arm to pull me close before he lowers his voice so that only I can hear him. "A woman is dead."

"So, you said." I roll my eyes. "And why, exactly, did you drag me all the way out here from my nice fancy dinner in the city to show me a dead stripper? Why aren't you investigating it?"

"Because I can't," he mumbles.

"What is that?" I ask with a huge, shit eating smile spreading across my face.

"Because I can't," he says louder through gritted teeth.

"And Wes?" I ask mildly.

"He can't either."

"And that would be because?" I hum.

"She was dancing for our party right before she died."

"Care to run that one by me again?" I ask.

"She was giving private dances to Jones's bachelor

party right before she took a break that she never came back from," he explains. I close my eyes and pinch the bridge of my nose.

"Please tell me that you weren't the last lap dance she gave before she bought it tonight, Lee." I need him to tell me that he's not going to be a suspect. I cannot handle having to arrest my brother.

"No. She didn't dance for me. The other girl did," he says answering my question. I take my first deep breath of the night before he soldiers on. "But Wes was."

"Excuse me?" I ask over the ringing in my ears but all I can think is what a waste of a perfectly good blowjob.

The rest, as they say, is history.

chapter 4

it's personal

THIS IS GOING TO be a long ass night.

"Show me the body." I sigh.

"It's right over here behind this dumpster."

I follow Liam over to the alleyway behind the club and sure enough, there's a dead girl back there. But that's not what's surprising.

The victim, who I would place at early to mid-thirties has blonde hair. Her eyes are closed and she's laying on her left side on the asphalt. While all that may seem fairly normal for your everyday homicide, that's where the "normal" ends.

Her eyes are closed and her hands are folded up in prayer under her cheek. At first glance you would think that she's just sleeping and her clothing choice is . . . *odd*.

"Is that what she was wearing earlier?" I ask wondering what kind of freaky kink these assholes I work with are into. When no one answers I look up from the young woman next to the dumpster and at the men standing around me. "Well?"

"No," Liam says after clearing his throat. "She dances here. Danced."

"I'm going to need all of you to head inside the club. No one leaves," I say after I sigh. Sometimes my job really sucks a monkey's testicle.

"Claire . . ."

"Nope," I say firmly. "I'll be inside in just a second." They all turn and tuck tail before heading back into the strip club like little boys who got a slap on the wrist from the school principal.

"Well it can't be said you guys don't know how to show a lady a good time," Emma says as she snaps on a pair of latex gloves that one of the crime scene techs handed to her. Liam looks back at her over his shoulder and blanches. I just stare at her.

"Really, Em?"

"What? Too soon?" She shrugs.

"Of course it's too soon!" I shout to the heavens as if Jesus and all the baby angels could help me. I start counting backwards from ten. I love Emma, but she's a little bit of a loose cannon.

"I meant us, loser!" she shouts. "Like, you, me, and Anna. Not the dead stripper."

"I could have a field day with all the shit you guys are slinging around tonight," Anna chimes in. "I'm going to schedule you all for in depth appointments this coming week. We need to log some serious couch time."

"Now will you look what you did?" I shout at Emma. She just shrugs in a so what fashion.

I sigh and roll my shoulders back. "What do you

have for me, Emma?"

"Well, she looks to be about mid-thirties, blonde hair, could be bleached but it doesn't look like it based on her roots. Victim appears to have been posed post-mortem," Emma shares.

"No immediate evidence on scene that suggests the victim was murdered here," one of the crime scene techs chimes in.

"I agree," Emma says. "There is bruising present at the back of the victim's shoulders that suggests the blood stopped pumping as she laid on her back, not her side. I won't know cause of death until I get her on my table, but there is also evidence of bruising on her neck."

"Strangulation?" I ask.

"On first look? Most likely," Emma agrees.

"That's messy," I mumble.

"Not messy," she corrects. "It's personal."

I stand there watching Emma as the crime scene techs comb the area for any evidence to the crime. Why was this woman murdered? Who would want to strangle her? I watch as Emma gently pulls the victim's lower lid down.

"Now that's interesting," she says softly.

"What?"

"She has violet eyes."

"And?" I ask.

"There's no contact lenses in her eyes. The color is natural."

"Okay," I hedge not sure what she's trying to say. I hope she just spits it out already. "What's so interesting about a woman with natural eye color?"

"It's not that she chooses to showcase her natural eye color that's interesting so much as the color itself," Emma explains. "I have never seen that natural color on anyone other than your dad, Liam . . . and *you*."

chapter 5

that's angel

"**D**ON'T BE RIDICULOUS." I roll my eyes.

"I'm not being ridiculous," Emma replies. "I'm serious. I have never seen purple eyes on anyone outside of your family."

"Well, now you have. She's not related to me, I can tell you that much!"

"I didn't say that she was related to you." She sighs. "I'm just saying, it's rare."

"Can we move along to the actual important facts of this case, please?" I'm tired and more than a little frustrated and it's beginning to show. I just wanted one freaking night off.

"Yes," she says.

"Fantastic." I'm letting my sarcasm show. It's not becoming but it's too late at night for me to care.

"The dress is interesting to say the least," Anna adds.

"It is," I say. "I'm not even sure I want to know why the killer would dress her up like a prairie person."

"It's almost like a doll," Emma muses as she takes in the floral dress with poufy sleeves and pin-tucked skirt underneath the white pinafore.

"It's almost like those people on the *Big Love* show we used to watch when we drank too much wine and were lonely—like now," Anna adds. I roll my eyes.

"I miss that show. It was a good one," I agree.

"I think I had an American Girl doll with the exact same outfit as a kid. Holy fuck, that's creepy," Emma shares.

"No kidding," I say.

"This case is definitely . . . interesting," Anna shares. "You're going to need a profiler on this case. What if it's a serial killer?"

"Shut your damn mouth and do not repeat those words until we have more than one body like this. This is creepy enough that the press will eat this shit up. I don't need any of those vultures hearing you say that shit right now," I bark out.

"Sorry," Anna says as she mimes locking her lips with a pretend key and throwing it away over her shoulder.

"Thank you." I nod.

"Anytime." She winks at me. God, I love my friends. They're crazy as hell, but I love them.

"I'm going to head on inside and interview the suspects," I say to the laughter of my friends.

"Oh, Liam will just love that," Anna says.

"Don't you know it." I laugh.

"Go easy on him." Anna bites down on her bottom lip like she wants to tell me more but doesn't.

"Never." I wink and Anna sighs.

"Give 'em hell, babe." Emma laughs.

I toss a wave over my head as I walk across the parking lot towards the back of the club where I pull open the back door. I hear the whispers from other dancers coming from the dressing rooms at the back of the building but as I pass, all talk stops. I know they are nervous about talking to the cops, but also scared because one of their own is dead.

There is a uniformed officer at the mouth of the hallway just after I pass the doors to the restrooms. I flag her down.

"Are these empty?" I ask pointing to the bathrooms.

"Yes, Detective. We cleared them."

"Good work. Thank you," I tell her. "I'm going to need a quiet booth or office to question the witnesses in."

"I'll get right on that, boss," she tells me as she moves to do just that. I think I like her.

I start to make my way into the main room when a large man, with sweat stains on the underarms of his white dress shirt and sweat beading all over his florid face, approaches me. Interesting. He could be in poor health or he could be nervous. But what about? That's the question. Could be he whacked her in the lot and he's a total mental case with the dresses and shit, but more than likely he's afraid the little stripper that bought it in his parking lot will hurt his bottom line. *Douchebag.*

"Excuse me, officer—" he starts before I stop to correct him. "Detective."

"Detective," he says as he rolls his eyes. Awesome. My favorite kind of witness. "What's going on here?"

"Who are you?" I ask as I tip my head to the side slightly in order to study him.

"I'm the manager of this club and you can't just shut me down for no reason," he demands.

"You're right, I can't." I nod my head casually.

"So, you're leaving," he tells me, not asks.

"No." I sigh. This is going to be a long fucking night. Lee so owes me. Wes too. I'm thinking cake cases from Liam and sexual favors from Wes. Yep, that sounds good.

"But, you just said!" he shouts sending little drops of spittle flying towards my face. Gross.

"I said," I say as I wipe a hand down my face. "That I can't shut you down for no reason. I can shut you down to investigate a homicide." I stop letting that little nugget of information sink in for a minute.

"What?" he shouts getting louder with each response. "Who? Why?"

"That's what I'm going to find out," I say.

"No," he shouts as he reaches for my arm. "This is my club. No bitch is going to come in here and shut me down without telling me what the hell is going on!" Just magical, this one is. I sigh gearing up to let him know that just because I have boobs doesn't mean I am any less of a detective. In fact, I'm the best, when Wes beats me to the proverbial punch.

Well, hell.

"Don't," Wes growls from behind him. "You let the nice detective go." I mean, it is kind of hot when he lets everyone know that I'm the boss.

The big, fat man releases my arm. "I meant no harm," he stammers.

"Sure, buddy. Just let her do her job so we can all go home." Wes winks at me.

"Yeah, that's a good idea," the club owner says. "I'll just be over . . . over there . . . *somewhere*," he trails off. I barely hold in my snicker at his hasty departure.

I walk back to the uniformed officer that was at the door and see her in a heated debate with a large man with the clear coil of an ear piece curling down from his left ear. He could be the bouncer, but I'm not sure. He's not secret service because there's no ugly ass black suit. He's in jeans and a gray t-shirt with muscles peeking out of every porthole.

"Hello again," I breeze through on a smile.

"Hello, Detective Goodnite," the officer says to me.

"Detective?" the bulky man asks on a raised eyebrow. *Asshole*.

You know, one day, it would be just peachy if everyone would just assume that I'm a lead detective and not, say, a cocktail waitress because I have a nice rack. Or someone's secretary because I have a vagina. I let out a quick breath before answering.

"Yes? Can I help you with something?"

"Yes, ma'am," he smiles a bright white smile as he holds out his hand. "I'm Chad Perry, the head of security here at the club."

"Fantastic," I say. "Why don't you come sit with me over here? You can give me the lay of the land."

I motion to the secluded booth that the officer and I had chosen for me to conduct my initial interviews. I turn and wink at her over my shoulder as I lead him away. She just rolls her eyes and laughs silently. Men! What will we ever do with them?

Chad slides into the booth with his back to the wall like he's Wild Fucking Bill Hickock and I kind of want to gag. Apparently, Wild Bill here thinks he's running this show. Well, that's just fine by me. He'll give me all the answers I need if he thinks he's helping out the little woman in the big scary job.

I slide into the booth beside him barely keeping my rolling eyeballs in check. The struggle is real, that's for sure. Chad snaps his fingers in the air and a woman in a string bikini and six-inch stilettos hustles on over. Just. Freaking. Charming.

"Sparkling water, Bubbles. Two," he barks before she turns and runs back towards the bar. When she returns just shy of two minutes later, I'm both impressed at her bar skills and sad for her. Bubbles sets two tall glasses of ice and sparkling water with lime wedges on the side of the glasses on the table.

"Thank you." I smile gently at her before she hustles away out of the eyesight of Wild Bill . . . I mean Chad.

"So, what do you have?" he demands as he takes a sip from his glass.

"A homicide," I say a little more cheerfully. He just looks at me and blinks once, twice . . .

"Is this your first one?" he asks not at all aware that his line of questioning is mildly offensive. Then again, I did see it coming a mile away.

"Come again?"

"Is this your first murder? Did you just pass the Detective's exam?" I sigh. What is he new here? It was only a few months ago that I made headline news—*national news*—as I investigated the kidnapping of a young boy. It also brought up a lot of unanswered questions in regard to my own kidnapping from years ago. But that's neither here nor there.

"No," I answer. "It's not my first homicide. I've been doing this for awhile now."

"That's hard to believe," he says thoughtfully as he studies my face. "You seem so . . . *young*. You're beautiful." Awe, fuck. I hope he doesn't hit on me.

"Well, thank you. What can you tell me about this club?" I ask hoping to change the subject to my questions.

"I almost went to the PD, you know, but decided the private sector was more suited for me. I'm a lone wolf," he says not taking my hints to stay on topic. And God damnit. He is hitting on me.

"You don't say," I mumble before moving on. "What can you tell me about the club?"

"It's a strip club," he tells me like I'm slow. Fuck this is going to be a long night.

"I meant about the operations," I pause to take a breath. Clearly, praying for strength to keep me from strangling this moron. "Who owns the club?"

"Bob Byrd," he says like that explains everything. I quirk one eyebrow in question. "Bob, the big guy running around being kind of a dick to everyone. He's the owner of the club." I had guessed as much, but Wild Bill and I had to start somewhere.

"And the dancers?" I asked.

"What about them?" Clearly, he's a prince among men.

"Do they like working here?" I ask.

"I don't know." He shrugs his overly muscle-bound shoulder. "I mean, who cares? Am I right?" He laughs. Uhh, no dude, you are, in fact, wrong. I barely keep myself from sharing those thoughts out loud.

"What do you mean by 'you don't know'? You work here as the head of security. Don't you know if the dancers are happy?"

"No," he shrugs his shoulders. "It's not my job to know if they're happy or to keep them that way."

"Did you ever date any of the dancers?" I ask changing tack.

"Define 'date'?" he smirks. Ugh, gross. I swallow the bile back down my throat. "I might sample the wares, but I don't stick around to see if they're happy in the long term—only in the short term." Yep, a real prince.

"Did the dancers ever complain about men that took too many liberties?"

"What do you mean?" he snaps. *Shit*. Me thinks the douchebag doth protest too much.

"I mean were there ever complaints about men that may have scared them?"

"There are always creeps in a strip club," he shrugs. Yeah, buddy, I'm looking at one of them right now.

I sigh. "Any issues with the parking lot?"

"We've had a light out for a week but nothing serious."

"Have you ever seen this woman before?" I ask as I pass him my phone with the picture I took of the victim's face.

"That's Angel," he says quietly.

"Angel?" I ask.

"She's—she was one of the dancers," he says. "She was on shift tonight for the bachelor party. She's one of the club's top performers so they bring her out to squeeze all of the money from the groom-to-be and his drunken buddies."

"Is Angel her real name?" I ask quietly trying to be gentle. There's something about Chad's mannerisms that tells me her death has struck him hard.

"Of course not. Don't be dumb." And he's back. "Her name is—*was*—Bonnie Bradley." And I have a name to match the face of a beautiful woman struck down before her time.

"Did she have an ex?"

"Don't they all?" He shrugs. Clearly, I'm not going to get anything else out of him. It's time to move on.

"Thank you for your time, Mr. Perry," I say as I stand from the booth.

"Wait," he says standing quickly. "I'd like to call you sometime, take you out and show you a good time." He winks.

"Thanks, but I'm seeing someone," I say politely.

"Your loss, babe."

"I'm sure," I say as I head to the back of the building towards the dressing rooms.

The crowds thin out as I move to the mouth of the hallway. The officer stands her ground and tips her chin to me ever so slightly. She and I see each other— the real woman there or at least as much of her as we might let others see—and tip our hats to the women we are and the women we have to pretend to be.

I pass by her and knock on the plain oak door that

blocks the entrance to the dancers' dressing room. After a beat, the door opens a crack and a woman peeks out enough that I can see just one pale, blue eye.

"Who are you?" she whispers.

"I'm Detective Claire Goodnite." I smile genuinely at her.

"I-I-I've seen you on the news," she says before pushing the door open just a little bit more. "C-c-c-come on in."

Once I pass through the door she pushes it shut and then throws the lock. I look around. There are at least a dozen women in this room in various stages of dress—or I should say, *undress*. Most are wearing robes of some kind.

"I'd like to ask you all a few questions, if that would be alright," I say softly as I pass by each woman, looking each one in the eye to silently show them that I will find out what happened to their friend. That I will protect their confidences and I will do my best to keep them safe. "Would that be alright? I can ask the female officer outside to step in if that would make you all feel better."

"Yeah, do that," the one who opened the door said.

I stick my head back out the door after she unlocks it for me. "Officer Alexander, could you please come here. Officer Bostwick, would you please take her post at the door. Thank you."

"You wanted to see me, boss?" Officer Alexander says as she steps around the crappy wooden door into the dressing room.

"Yes." I smile kindly at her and the other women in the room. "We all think it would be best if you were in here while I interview the witnesses." I stress the word witnesses because I'm not really sure what to call them and I don't want to offend them in any way.

"Sounds like a plan," Officer Alexander states.

"Ladies, this is Officer Alexander," I say out loud for the whole room to hear.

"You can call me Jasmine," she says.

"Jasmine," the gatekeeper woman by the door tests out. "I'm Hoots. That's Serenity and Bubbles."

"Nice to meet you, ladies," I say politely.

"Glad to know you," Jasmine shares to the chorus of same here's around the women in the room.

"Now, what can you all tell me about Angel?" I ask after I settle in, leaning back against a makeup vanity with big lights.

"She was nice enough," Bubbles shares.

"Did you know her well?"

"She helped me with my Algebra homework before the club opened."

"How old are you?" I ask Bubbles.

"Eighteen," she says as she looks at the floor. "Said I was the same age as her daughter."

"So, she had a daughter. Did she have any other children?"

"A son. He's nineteen and in the Army," Hoots informs from the door.

"And another one who's ten," Serenity says softly from the corner.

"And a husband?" I ask.

"Ha!" she cackles. "The sack of shit that knocked her up never married her."

"Would he ever harm her in anyway?" I ask.

"No, he was a little weasel who liked the dog track just a little too much and couldn't be bothered with things like regular work enough to pay child support or even hold down a job. But he wasn't mean."

"And she loved him," Serenity says.

"Serenity is still young enough to believe in that line of bullshit," Hoots shares causing both Jasmine and I to bite our lips to keep from laughing.

"Am not!" Serenity yells.

"Was there anyone Angel was afraid of?" I ask after the ladies who are obvious friends settle down.

"No," Hoots shares.

"I can't think of anyone," Bubbles adds.

"Were there any customers that gave her—*or you, for that matter*—the creeps?"

"Honey, they're all creeps in one way or another," Hoots shares from the door and I can't help but think about the fact that tonight's resident creeps were my colleagues, my boyfriend, and my brother. *Lucky me!*

"No one that bothers you?" I ask.

"Well, Bob is a jerk who only cares about the talent in terms of the bottom line. He likes his paychecks too much to care about anything else."

"Yeah. He's a jerk, but he's harmless," Bubbles says.

"Now, Chad is a little shit but he's good with his cock so we've all seen the ceiling of the backseat of his car a time or two, but nothing past that," Hoots says candidly.

"You'll find who did this to our Angel?" Serenity asks me in a child-like voice.

"I'm going to do my very best," I promise her.

"Should we be worried?" Hoots asks when I push off the table top to make my way to the door.

"You should always be cautious," I hedge. "I can't divulge any pertinent facts of the case at this time," I say as the words *serial killer* flash in neon lights across my brain. So far, I only have one body on my hands, but God damn Anna for suggesting otherwise. Now it's all I freaking see.

"Remember, ladies," Jasmine says in a confident voice. "It's that dipshit Chad's job to see to your safety. Make him walk you to your cars at night—*every night*. Don't go out those back doors alone. Be aware of your surroundings. And take my self-defense class at the community center on Wednesday nights." I quirk a brow in her direction. She just shrugs her shoulder in a so what motion.

"Thank you, Officer," I say once we've cleared the dressing room. She just tips her head in a nod before resuming her post outside their door. I think I like her.

I make my way back to my booth and stop halfway across the room at a table where most of my male colleagues are sitting. I sigh. What a bunch of beautiful morons. Only these guys would be at a strip club for a bachelor party where one of the dancers got killed.

"One at a time, come on over to that table and give me your statements gentlemen," I say as I point towards my booth.

"Linda is going to fucking kill me," Jones whines. He's drunk as a skunk and crying with his face in his hands like a big baby—not like the two-hundred-eighty-pound Mack truck of a police officer we all know and love.

"Linda isn't going to kill you," I reassure him. But honestly, if I was Linda, I would so kill him.

"I'm going to fucking kill you if you don't quit God damned crying right this minute," Liam grumbles under his breath. There's that family resemblance we know so well. The thought sobers me as I remember the bright purple eyes that Lee and I also share—along with our victim.

"I'm just going to be right over there," I say as I motion to my table.

I walk across the room and sit down. Bubbles brings me an unopened bottle of water before moving along without saying a word. I think she likes me. Look at me making friends and shit.

Liam slides into the booth across from me.

"Tell me everything you've got," he demands.

"I'm not sure that's what should happen here, Lee."

"Don't feed me that line of bullshit, Goodnite. I'm your Captain and you'd do well to remember it," he threatens me. Always with the threats, this one. I sigh.

"How can I forget it!" I snap. "You remind me every day, including when we're at Mom and Dad's!"

"This is a homicide, Claire," he says as he softens his tone of voice towards me.

"I know that," I respond after taking a deep breath. "But you're a witness here. Why don't you start at the beginning and tell me everything that happened tonight?"

He sighs. I know that he sees the truth in what I'm saying. The last thing we need is questionable police work on this case after what happened with the Donovan case. Five months ago, I caught a missing persons case. A six-year-old boy, Anthony Donovan, was reported missing from his modest suburban home where he lived with his mom, sister, and step-dad. The case should have been easy, but it was anything but.

He sighs, running his hand through his hair before answering. "We went out to dinner at the Bullpen before walking over here."

"So, you guys went to the nastiest sports bar in town for beer and wings before coming over here for more booze and naked ladies?" I ask, my eyes narrowed.

He looks nervously back over his shoulder at the table of guys before looking back at me. Well, that's not a good sign. I wonder just how much looking at the pretty, naked ladies my boyfriend did.

"It's not like that," my brother says pointedly homing in on my weak moments. Wes and I are so new, I can't help but wonder when the love bubble will burst. There's that ugly word again.

"Okay," I say thoughtfully.

"I mean it, Claire," he says, his voice low and full of meaning.

I sigh. "I know. Tell me what happened."

"We came back here and had a few drinks. We bought Jones a few lap dances to send him off into marital bliss with."

"I will never understand why men think having another naked woman rub all over them before settling down is a good idea."

"Claire." Lee stares me down.

"What?" I ask holding my arms out.

"That's it, Claire," he sighs again. I wear on his patience, I know that already. "We just sat there, drank, talked, and watched some pretty girls."

"And when you found the girl?" I questioned.

"We had gone out to smoke, she was laying by the dumpster. I checked her pulse, but I already knew that I wouldn't find one. Wes called it in. Then I called you. The rest, as we say, is history."

"Okay," I say. "If you think of anything else, let me know."

"I will," he tells me. "Once you clear us, I'd appreciate being caught up to speed."

"You got it," I tell him before he stands up and walks away.

I crack the seal on the cap of the water bottle that Bubbles had brought me and looked down at it. I can feel the frown pulling at my brows. She brought me a bottle—a *sealed* bottle—not a glass like Chad had ordered for me. I can't help but wonder if it's for safety or protection. Protection from who? Chad? Bob? And then I wonder how many times the girls here had to watch out for things like that.

"Hey, Cruz." I smile at the man as he sits down across from me. He smiles brightly back at me.

Abraham Cruz is the newest detective to arrive at our station. He's from somewhere in the Midwest. I can't remember where. He replaced Hudson, a seasoned detective who broke cover and took a bullet for me a few months ago. Last I heard, Hudson was chasing a redheaded Game Warden with big boobs and brass balls all over East Texas. And if rumors were true, he married her one night in Vegas after one too many drinks. Good for him.

"Hey, Claire," Cruz says. "Fancy meeting you

here."

"I know, right?" I laugh. "I should be eight martinis deep with Anna and Emma."

"That sounds like fun," he says quietly but his words have my brain turning. I tip my head to the side to study him. I wonder if he has a thing for Emma or Anna. That has to be it.

"They're both single, you know," I whisper. His smile dims a bit. "Emma and Anna, I mean."

"Yeah. I know." He smiles at me again.

"So, what can you tell me about tonight?" I ask.

"We started at the Bullpen. Jones got drunk. We came here. Jones got more drunk. O'Connell and the Captain went out to smoke and found the dancer with the purple eyes," he explains. But all I see is red. I can't believe both of those assholes told me that they had quit smoking when they, in fact, did not quit smoking! "Come to think of it, they're a lot like yours."

"If you think of anything else, call me?" I ask him, even though he already knows to.

"Of course," he says as he shoots me a crooked grin. God the guys in this unit love to mess with me. I should kick all their asses.

He stands from the booth and touches the tip of his index finger to the back of my hand where it rests on top of the table and heads back over to the guys. What the fuck was that? But I don't have time to contemplate it as Wes walks up to the booth and sits down.

"What the fuck was that all about?" he quietly roars.

"Umm, excuse me?" I retort.

"What the fuck is going on with you and Cruz?"

"Nothing," I say as I narrow my eyes on him. "Why are you being this way?"

"Because you're mine, Claire," he growls. "Learn it, live it, love it, baby, because it ain't changing."

"God, you're such an asshole." I roll my eyes at him.

"And you love every bit of it." He winks at me. There's that word again.

"Not currently," I sigh. "Look, I need to know what happened tonight so I can go out and catch a killer. Whatever drunken jealousy this is," I say as I motion back and forth between us with my hand, "I don't have time for it."

"I'm not drunk," he says. "I know what I saw."

"Okay," I say in an effort to redirect. "What happened tonight?"

"We went to the Bullpen and ate too many chicken wings, Jones drank too much beer and told everyone who would listen 'What an angel his Linda is' and then we came here. He got more drunk. There were dancers. Lee and I went out to smoke which I already know you're pissed about but we like to smoke when we drink," he shrugs his impressive shoulders. "It's a Navy thing. Then we saw the girl. Lee checked her and she was for sure dead. So, I called it in and he called you. Now here we are."

"That's it?" I ask frustrated that not one professional can give me anything to go on.

"That's it," he confirms.

"Alright. Thanks, Wes."

"Come see me before you leave," he demands as he stands from the table. "I love you, Claire."

I sigh. "I know."

Wes walks his tall body back to the table with all of the guys. I'm not ashamed to admit that I watch him go and enjoy the view. He's kind of an asshole sometimes, but he's my asshole so there's that.

"Well?" Bob, the club owner snaps drawing me out of my Wes induced fantasy.

"Well, what?" I ask.

"Did one of those guys do it?" he asks as he points to the table of cops.

"Uhh, no," I say looking at him like he's lost his damn mind.

"Yes, one of them did," he tells me.

"You do know that that is a table of seasoned cops, right? They're ultimate professionals."

"And one of them killed my dancer. Find out who. He's costing me money." It's official, Bob Byrd has a major fucking screw loose.

"I'll do my best," I say before he turns on his heels and storms away.

Jones drags his heels, sniveling as he comes right up to the booth I'm sitting in. I motion for him to take a seat across from me but instead he slides in next to me and rests his big, bald head on my shoulder as he cries his heart out, wiping his nose on my shoulder. It just goes to show that the bigger they are on the outside, the bigger babies they actually are on the inside.

"Linda is going to be so fucking mad . . ." he wails.

Oh, fuck me running. I am not equipped to handle this shit.

I look up wide eyed to the table of cops and they all stare at me with merriment and mischief twinkling in their eyes. Those fucking bastards. They knew that Jones was way too drunk to give a statement.

"Linda will never forgive me! What do I do?" Jones asks as he wipes his nose on the back of his hand before nuzzling into my shoulder.

"I'm sure it'll all work out, Jones."

"You're so nice and sweet and smart and pretty. No wonder O'Connell likes to give you the business."

"Jones—" I say but am cut off by the raucous laughter of the morons I work with.

"And oh man, was the Captain pissed when he found out you had banged the Fed. I mean *pissed* pissed." Jones drunkenly rambled on.

"I got it, Jones," I say hoping to move this train right the hell along.

"But I'm glad to see it all worked out." He nods.

"Me too."

"I'm sleepy, Goodnite. Do you think I can just sleep he—" but he doesn't finish the sentence before a snore rips from his face. Boy am I glad I'm not him. Jones is going to wish he was dead in the morning.

I crook my index finger at the table of my friends and colleagues in a come here motion and they all shake their heads and mouth, "Nu-uh." But I don't care.

"Come here right now or I will have you all arrested and thrown in the drunk tank tonight! I hear Big Betsy was picked up tonight for solicitation. Last I remembered she had a thing for Wes and Lee. Isn't that right, Jasmine?"

"Absolutely," she smiles knowing that we can have some fun with them too.

"Coming!" they all shout as the rush over to grab

Jones off of my person.

"Don't leave town, boys. You'll be hearing from me," I say. With that I push up from the booth and walk back outside.

Emma is finishing up clearing the scene.

"How's it going out here, ladies?" I ask them.

"Oh, you know, it's going," Anna says thoughtfully. "How's it going in there?"

"They are all a bunch of idiots," I mumble under my breath.

"That good, huh?" Emma asks gleefully. Apparently, it wasn't that much of a mumble.

"The guys are morons. Wes and Lee are smoking again claiming 'it's a Navy thing,' so there's that. The owner and the bouncer are both the creepiest of creeps and the dancers are worried about something but won't tell me what."

"Well," Emma says as she closes the back of the Medical Examiner van. "I'd say their fear has something to do with the fact that one of their friends bought it behind the shitty strip club where they work and was laid out to look like she was sleeping dressed like a fucking prairie person."

"As always," Anna drawls. "Emma is direct and to the point."

"Thanks, babe." Emma smiles brightly and I'm reminded that with her blonde hair and blue eyes, she could easily be a movie star. "I'm uhh . . . just going to take our girl back to the morgue," she says looking at something over my shoulder.

"Yeah, sure, babe. I'll talk to you later," I say distractedly.

"I'll call you when I know more," she says before climbing into the passenger seat of the van. I turn and see Liam watching her every move.

"We're going to have to talk about this," Wes says quietly from behind me.

"Actually, we're not," I say not even turning to look at him.

"Claire—" he starts.

"No," I stop him as I turn around. "This is my job. And I'm not arguing with you or Liam about it. Again."

"We need to talk about this," he says again.

"Not until you're clear. We're not talking about anything. By the book, Wes."

"You can't possibly think I did this!" he snaps.

"And you can't possibly think that my job isn't on the line after the Donovan case," I snap back. "I can't risk this case by playing favorites, Wes."

"I'm not asking you to play favorites, honey. I just need you to know that I love you. I'm here for you. I need to know that you trust me enough to know that I didn't kill a stripper—that I just met by the way." He calmly explains.

"I know," I say as he pulls me into his arms. It's highly unprofessional but I'm tired and I needed the comfort of him for just a minute. But once there in his embrace, I realize he smells like sweat, bourbon, and someone else's perfume. Suddenly Wes's hold isn't so comforting.

"Don't be mad, baby," he says when I pull out of his arms.

"I'm not. I just need to do my job and wrap this case up. There's something about it that's bothering me."

"Honey, the whole thing should bother you. The way she was laid out—" He shudders. "It was bad."

"It is bad," I say and then I open and close my mouth trying to decide if the words that are choking me should be the words that come out of my mouth. "I just—"

"*Don't*," his voice sounds harshly in the dark. "Don't you dare use a bad case as an excuse to run. You have been looking for a reason to for months and I hate it." He tears at his hair with his hands.

"Well, it's true." When will Wes see that, while we . . . care for each other, there is no possible way that this relationship can go anywhere but to a terrible and tragic end.

"The fuck it is!" he shouts.

"You know it's true, Wes. It shouldn't be this—"

"No." He cuts me off.

"Complicated." I finish.

"No, it's not, baby," he pleads. "It's really fucking easy. It's you and it's me. That's all it needs to be."

"Look," I say as I pull from his hold. "I have to go. I'll see you later." And then I leave him there, behind a shitty strip club as I walk to Anna. I climb into the cab that she has procured for us to get home. I let the door shut behind me with a resounding click and hope against all hope that it wasn't the final straw in the Claire and Wes story. No matter what I may have told him only moments before, I'm not ready for it to end.

chapter 6

cold-blooded killer

"ARE YOU ALRIGHT?" ANNA asks.

It's a simple question but the answer is complicated. The fact of the matter is, I just don't know. What started out as a night of fun ended in one of the creepiest murder scenes I have ever seen—and my last case was a doozy.

"Claire?" she asks again as our cab flies down the road. "Are you okay?"

"I don't know."

The cab pulls to a stop in front of my apartment building and I shove open the door like I'm jumping from a sinking ship. I know that Anna is going to want to talk about the case and how it makes me feel. That scene with Wes and how that makes me feel. *All the freaking bullshit and how it makes me feel*. But tonight, I just need to process everything and she can shrink my head tomorrow. But as for right now, I'm not even sure how that makes me feel.

But I also know that she won't wait that long. Anna

can hold her own with Emma and I. Even with Liam and Wes. She won't let my bullshit slide and we both know it.

"I'll call and check in when I get home," she says quietly.

"I wouldn't expect anything less."

"Count on it." She smirks.

"I always do," I say suddenly feeling tired. Defeated.

"You know that I love you Claire, right?" she asks me.

"I love you too, Anna. I'll be okay. I promise. Go home and find some poor asshole to torture on your internet dating sites."

"Hey! Mr. Right is out there," she says thoughtfully before adding. "He's probably just being held hostage in some war-torn nation." At that I smile.

"Goodnight," I say as I shut the door.

"Goodnight, Goodnite!" she shouts out the window as the cab rolls out into the night making me laugh.

I climb the steps to my second story apartment and unlock the row of locks down the door. After the last case, my dad insisted on adding some unnecessary hardware to my door. I love him, so I humor him and lock every last one of them.

I repeat the process as soon as I enter my apartment with a sigh. I look at the worn couch and know that if I sit down, I won't be getting back up until morning. I'm so exhausted. So, I walk straight through to my bathroom, brush my teeth, and scrub off my makeup.

. It takes longer than usual because I caked it on like a fancy hooker for girls' night out.

I twist my long hair up into a messy bun with a rubber band before padding my way down the hall to my bedroom. I could put on pajamas, but I could also just lay down and sleep in my clothes. Then I remember the crime scene that pulled me away from a fun night of dinner and drinks with my friends and I feel dirty—*unclean*. So, I strip out of my clothes and toss them in a pile by the door. Once I'm naked, I crawl under the sheets ready to drift off to sleep, but my phone has other plans.

Or I should say, my meddling best friend on the other end of the line has alternate plans.

"Hello?" I answer.

"Hello, Claire," she says. "I'm home."

"I'm in bed," I inform her.

"Will you be okay?" she asks. "I can head back over."

"No, I'm fine. I just need some sleep and to hit the trail again tomorrow," I reassure her.

"And Wes?" she asks casually but I can tell her question is anything but.

"I don't know," I say thoughtfully. "What I told him is true. We feel too complicated. Like it should be easier and it's not."

"Do you love him?" she asks, saying that little four-letter word again.

"Yes," I answer with the truth in my heart without hesitation.

"Then it will either work out or it won't," she says sagely.

"Thank you so much for your expert opinion, Dr. Spock." I laugh.

"Dr. Spock was a baby doctor you moron. Shut up and go to sleep." She laughs.

"You too," I respond softly.

"Goodnight, Goodnite."

"Goodnight, dumbass. I love you." And then I hang up, placing my phone on the nightstand before I drift off to sleep.

Wes and Liam are so mean! I can't believe they won't let me hangout with them. I bet they're just afraid that I'll tell mom and Mrs. O'Connell about the magazines they're hiding with the girls in bikinis in them.

I'm stomping through the woods behind our house. I don't need those gross boys to have some fun. And those boys are gross! They smell weird and put on too much stinky spray stuff when they think I'm not looking.

I just make it to the street on the other side of the trees from our house when a white van pulls up next to me. I hear my mom in my head telling me not to talk to strangers. I feel my eyes going wide as he steps out of the van.

"Claire!" he says and I wonder how he knows my name. "There you are. I need your help!"

"What do you need help with?" I ask.

"I'm so glad you asked, Claire," he says my name again like he says it all the time. It's weird but I don't think too much about it. "My puppy, Millie, got out. She's missing. Can you help me find her?"

"I don't know. I should probably go back home . .

." I say.

"No!" he shouts and it startles me and I jump a little. His eyes widen when he notices my reaction. "I need you to look for her while I drive around. I'll give you this candy bar if you help me . . ." he offers, holding up my most favorite kind. I instantly grab for it, but he pulls it back.

"Okay, what does she look like?" I ask.

He smiles a creepy smile showing all of his teeth, but I open the front door and get in the van. He hands me the candy bar and I realize that I don't even know what his name is . . .

"She's little and fluffy and white . . ." he trails off as I dig into the sweets my mom never lets me eat before dinner. Ever!

All of a sudden, my head feels funny and my ears feel full of cotton like last summer when I got an infection from swimming too much. I open my mouth to tell him something is wrong, but my words don't work. They won't come out! I turn my head to look at him, a scream stuck in my broken mouth. He just smiles his big, creepy smile and everything goes black . . .

When I wake up, I look down, I'm wearing a funny old timey dress just like the one Angel was wearing and I know that it's my turn to die.

A scream rents the air. It's my scream but I can't seem to stop. I can't make myself leave this dream. And the worst part is knowing that I am alone and I have no one to blame but myself.

"Claire." I hear the voice I most want to hear say my name as my dream takes on a cruel twist. I whimper but I don't open my eyes. Someone shakes me. "Claire," he says louder as he pulls me free from the dream.

"Wes," I sigh.

"I'm here, baby. I told you I would always be here." He pulls me into his arms and I realize that he's laying in my bed. Wes came home. Well, to my home, but right now I don't care. I wrap my arms around his neck and crush my mouth to his.

"Wes," I plead when I pull back to look in his eyes.

"I'm here, baby."

"I need you." And I do. I need Wes.

He rolls me to my back before using his knees to slide my legs apart. I instantly pull my own knees up high and wide as he settles in between my thighs.

"Wes, I need you," I plead.

"I need you too, baby. I need you so much." And then he touches his forehead to mine and slides in to the hilt.

Wes braces his weight on his forearms as he slowly pumps his cock into my waiting body. He frames my face with his rough palms and I love it. I love getting lost in the feel of his hard body, the coarse hair on his chest, as he moves against me—*with me*.

This is everything that I need.

The way Wes makes love to me in the middle of the night, chasing away the bogeyman, is all that I need— that it's all that I'll *ever* need—I can't help but feeling like maybe he was right after all. Maybe it's not complicated at all, maybe it's real fucking simple.

I arch my back against Wes, my arms and legs grip around his body as my pussy grips his cock tight. I let out his name on a gasp as I climax and he follows me right over the edge into bliss.

"I love you, Claire," he says just as the gray of sleep takes me under, my body still wrapped around his. I can't help but think the words that most need to be said but I know that it'll wait until morning.

I love you too.

Too bad that it really wouldn't wait.

chapter 7

that stings

*B*EEP . . . *BEEP* . . . *BEEP.*
My alarm blares from beside my bed. I reach over to silence it on the nightstand when the bulky arms that are wrapped around my body squeeze the breath right out of me.

"I meant what I said last night." His already deep voice is burred by sleep. The sound of it next to my ear makes a shiver wrack up my spine.

"I know," I whisper.

"Good," is his only response as he coasts one palm up my belly to cup my breast where he casually circles his thumb around my nipple.

I bite my lip to hold in a moan as I arch back against his hard body.

Wes drives his other hand down my belly to between my legs where he finds me wet and wanting. I grip his hand between my thighs.

"Claire," he rumbles next to my ear as he circles my clit with his fingers but I don't want to talk this morning. There are too many things that need to be said and I'm not ready to say them. So, I tip my hips back against his groin.

"Shut up and fuck me, Wes," I demand.

"Yes, ma'am," he says before he slides his cock into my waiting body.

"Yes," I purr.

Our bodies move as one as we rock together. Our coupling is as loving as it is frenzied and urgent. I'm glad that I can't see his face. I know what I would see there and we both know that I'm not ready. I have been barely hanging on to this relationship business since I was shoved over the falls by a deranged murderer five months ago.

And we both know that Wes wants more. He has been silently guiding me towards holy matrimony the same way one would try to tame a skittish colt.

He circles his fingers faster as he picks up pace. Thank God. The coarse hair on his thighs abrading my legs as I rock my hips against him, meeting him thrust for thrust before finally throwing my head back to rest on his shoulder as I claw at the sheets and the pillows in front of me with my free hand. The other is hanging on to Wes's at my center like a lifeline. My body tightens from head to my toes and I come. Wes rocks into my body one more time before planting himself there and following me over the edge, growling out his release.

"Claire," he groans with his face to the side of my neck.

"I love you too," I whisper hoping he doesn't hear it but by the stiffening of his body as every muscle contracts, I know that he does.

We lay there, neither one of us wanting to break the spell by moving—for what seems like an eternity when the alarm on Wes's phone blares bursting our love bubble.

"Claire—" he starts.

"You need to go," I tell him.

"I don't want to go."

I sigh. "Let's just get this day over with. We can talk later."

"Claire—" he starts.

"Not yet, Wes," I plead. "I'm not ready yet."

He sighs in frustration over my lack of enthusiasm regarding our relationship as he slides his softening cock from my hold before throwing the sheets back and prowling off to the bathroom.

Our love bubble is officially toast.

I hear the water kick on in the shower and I wonder if it's too cowardly of me if I hide under the covers until he leaves my apartment. Deciding that sounds like a fantastic idea I grab the blankets he tossed away and am just starting to pull them back up the bed when a firm hand clasps my ankle and tugs me down the bed.

And I scream like a little girl. Some badass I am.

Wes tosses me over his shoulder like a fireman and I meet the glorious vision of his firm backside. I think I might be drooling just a bit and my eyes glaze over at the sight of all that sculpted muscle. He might be approaching advanced age at his thirty-eight years, but Wes still has a banging body.

I'm distracted by my thoughts when his large hand smacks my ass as it hangs in the air. I let out and embarrassing *Eep!*

"God damnit, Wes!" I shout.

"You are not going to chase me away every time you're a chicken shit," he says as he swats me again.

"Damnit! That stings."

"You get to be scared," he says as he swats me again and the soothes the sting with his palm. "I'm scared too. But you will not run from me."

"I'll do what I want, you big bossy bastard!" I shout as I try and protect my ass which—if I'm honest—doesn't actually hurt.

"I love you and your colorful use of alliteration," he says softly as he steps into the shower and the frigid water slices over my skin.

"Holy fuck this is freezing!"

"I know," he tells me with a smirk after he lets my naked body slide down his. "I can't go into work with a raging hard-on. They'll never let me live it down."

"That doesn't sound like my problem," I pout.

"It's not. But when you're around, I'm always hard. Fuck, I can be sitting at my desk and remember something funny you said or how beautiful you looked the night before and bam! I'm hard."

"I think that might be a compliment wrapped in vulgarity," I pout.

"It is. I love all of you, baby. The good and the bad," he says smoothly.

"Bad?" I purr. "How bad?" I ask as I wrap my hand around his cock and stroke him with my fist. The cold water doesn't seem to be helping his . . . *problem.*

I let him go to fill my hands with shampoo and start washing my hair. Wes swats my hands aside and gently tends to my long mane. I love how tender he can be when it's just us. It's one of the many different facets of Wes that I seem to be falling more in love with each one every day.

We take our time washing each other in the cold spray, using our hands and our mouths to say the things that I know that I'm not ready for—at the same time Wes is eager to shove us over the cliff.

And the truth in the moment is clear—we want the same thing—to love each other.

Wes shuts the taps off when the soap is gone and the water runs clear. We dry off and silently dress for our day. We stop on the landing outside my front door as I pull it tight and turn the key in my many locks.

"I have to come into the station to sign a statement for Liam," he says before curling his body around mine and landing the mother of all kisses on my lips. "Don't run."

"Okay," I whisper against his lips.

"Okay." His voice vibrates against my mouth. "I'll see you later." And then he kisses me one more time before letting me go.

We walk down the stairs to the parking lot and turn in separate directions for our vehicles. I'm in a hurry so I don't stop and look back. Later, I would wish that I had because if I had seen the look of love and longing on his face my response when tested later would be different. *Maybe*.

chapter 8

blink of an eye

FUCK I NEED COFFEE.

All I could think about the whole drive to the station was how bad I wanted coffee. I didn't drink a ton last night because over indulging in booze scares the hell out of me. I have seen way too many good cops go down dark paths because they couldn't handle the really shitty parts of the job so they chose to cope with liquor and sex. We're all capable of it. Add in my own tale of woe—the mystery surrounding my own kidnapping twenty-four years ago—and the potential is there for me to go off the rails for sure.

So, I had a few mixed drinks with the girls over dinner, but it never went past that. I was sober by the time our cab made it back to New Jersey. A good thing since I came face to face with one of the creepiest cases I've ever seen as soon as my feet touched the asphalt of the parking lot.

But now I need coffee. I don't just want it, *I need it*. It's my life's blood and it might actually be what flows through my veins.

I pull into the parking lot of the station and take a deep breath as I pull the glass door open. I love it here. In fact, I grew up here. My dad was the Captain at this very station when Liam and I were growing up. No one was surprised when Lee followed in his footsteps, yet everyone acted like I had said that I like to kill baskets of puppies on the weekends when I chose to do the same.

Life can be a real bitch sometimes.

I walk straight past my desk, dutifully ignoring the massive stack of inter-office messages and mail and head straight for the kitchenette in the back where the magical coffee maker lives. I pull a cup from the stack and pour myself a cup of the good stuff. I guzzle it down like a hooker on her knees and give not one fuck that it's steaming hot.

I set my cup down and let out a deep sigh. "Thank God."

"You alright there, Claire?" I hear from in front of me. I didn't notice anyone follow me into the kitchen because I had a one-track mind and that track was on coffee, glorious, magical coffee.

"Just peachy," I sigh again before opening my eyes and taking in Abraham Cruz. His blue eyes twinkle as he takes me in. I pretend like I don't notice his eyes track down my body before slowing on all the places a bathing suit might cover.

"Understandable," he says as he nods to the coffee cup that I am refilling. "It was a pretty rough night."

"That it was," I agree. "Coffee?" I hold up the coffee carafe in my hand offering him a warm up.

"If that's all you're offering," he mumbles. *Interesting*. And unwelcome.

"That it is," I say on a tight smile.

"Then, yes, coffee." He holds out his cup and I fill it up for him. "Thank you."

"Anytime." I smile at him from behind my cup. He's a nice guy although nobody really knows him very well yet. We will. We don't let detectives go rogue. Around here, there are no lone wolves.

"I have to say, Detective, I like the jeans and t-shirts you wear here—but that dress you wore last night was amazing." He winks.

"An LBD is hardly crime fighting gear," I say in a mock stern tone.

"I don't know what a LBD is, but hard-ons are the only thing anyone was fighting."

His comments are crude and inappropriate, but they make me laugh. I've been one of the guys for ages. I avoid flirtations like this because I wouldn't want to give anyone the wrong idea. But now that I'm with Wes, *really with Wes*, and everyone knows that I'm taken, I can engage in ridiculous flirting which is harmless and fun.

"An LBD is a little black dress and you're an idiot." I laugh.

"You wound me, Goodnite," he says as he clutches his chest in an overly dramatic attempt to show me that he's heart broken.

"Somehow I think that you'll survive."

He opens his mouth to respond but Liam bellowing from within his office interrupts him.

"Goodnite! My office. Now!"

I sigh. "Duty calls."

"Good luck with that one, Goodnite."

I make my way down the hall to Lee's office and knock on the door.

"Get your ass in here," he shouts just before I push the heavy door open. I'm barely through when I'm grabbed by my arm—ambushed really—and shoved against the wall. A large, hulking mass of angry man crowds me in and stares me down.

"What the fuck was that?" Wes snaps.

"What the fuck was what?" I ask. What the hell is he so mad about? I just left him like an hour ago. He's barely had time to check in at his field office before heading to this station house. So, I'm not sure what the hell he could be so mad about now.

"You know what," he seethes.

I blink. "No, actually, I have no idea what you're talking about." And I don't. Truly.

He seems to weigh my words for a minute before asking me, point blank, "Are you interested in Detective Cruz?"

"What?" I ask shocked. I'm truly shocked. "Why would you even think that?"

"Because I saw you with him on my way in. You had that look on your face you get right after you come," Wes says pointing right at my face.

"Too much information about my sister in my office, asshole. Thanks," Liam grumbles from his seat at his desk. I watch him over Wes's shoulder as he shoots Wes's back the bird. *Nice.*

"Answer me," Wes demands softly as he uses a fingertip to push me back to face him by my chin.

"Nothing happened," I explain.

"And the face?" he questions.

"Jesus Christ," Liam gripes from across the room.

"I was drinking coffee. It was my first cup of the morning after a long night. I would have had one—or eight—at home but someone distracted me." I give him a pointed, you-know-what-I'm-talking-about look that obviously speaks volumes.

"Just shoot me," Liam groans.

"Gladly," I say over Wes's shoulder.

"And Cruz? It looked like you were flirting."

"I was, kind of. Better?" I ask.

"How is that better?" he gripes.

"Because it was nothing. A little harmless flirting as a joke because everyone knows that I'm with you. All hope of getting into my panties is lost for the fore-seeable future." I nod with my eyes wide in all serious-ness.

"For the foreseeable future?" He asks, his tone deadly.

"Yes," I reassure him.

"That is ridiculous!" Wes shouts picking his mad back up to speed. "None of this shit would happen if you would just marry me!"

"Marry you? Are you insane?" I shout.

"No. I need something to go on. You say everyone knows that you're taken, but *I* don't even know that you're taken. You have to give me something."

"Are you saying that you're not taken? Are you seeing other people?" I ask feeling like my heart is about to shatter.

"No! I *am* taken, but it feels like I belong to a woman with one foot out the door." That is an alarmingly accurate depiction. "Marry me. Be mine."

"Actually," Lee wades in. "This is good. This would solve a lot of my problems."

"How does my marrying your lunatic best friend solve any of your problems?"

"Easy." He shrugs. "You become Wes's problem, not mine."

"Ugh," I groan as I roll my eyes so hard my head hurts. "You're both morons."

"So that's a no?" Liam asks for Wes.

"Yes!"

"She said yes!" Lee shouts.

"I said yes, I'm saying no, you assholes."

"You're saying no?" Wes asks, his voice low and angry.

"I'm saying this is ridiculous. I am not marrying you because you're a jealous Neanderthal. Ask me again some other time when you actually mean it and I *might* say yes."

"She's going to kill me," Wes muses to Liam. "I'm surprised my hair isn't a shock of white by now or that I haven't keeled over from a massive coronary yet."

"The day is still young, asshole," I cheer.

"Welcome to my world, brother," Liam commiserates.

"Har-de-har-har, assholes." They both look at me expectantly. "What?"

"Nothing."

"No reason."

"Well was there an actual reason why you called me in here or was it just to be a bunch of crazies?"

"I want an update on the Angel case," Liam commands. His posture is rigid showing his full power and importance in this office. This is Captain Goodnite.

"She's dead," I say.

"No shit, Sherlock," he grumbles. "Tell me more."

"That's it," I tell him. "I just fucking got here."

"Well, what did you find out last night?" Liam asks as an odd look crosses over Wes's face briefly. It's gone in the blink of an eye.

"That you guys are a bunch of assholes who drank too much and acted like a bunch of morons. Oh, and Jones is in love with his soon-to-be-wife. He is included in the drunken morons category."

"You have nothing," he states.

"Bupkis," I agree.

"Better get back to the salt mines then."

"Gladly." I slip out from behind Wes and bow towards Liam. "Always a pleasure, douche canoe." I take a step towards the door when Wes stops me with a hand on my upper arm.

"Wait," he says.

"What is it?" I ask.

"Are you mad?" He looks concerned. He acted like an idiot but I'm kind of used to it by now.

"No," I answer and he visibly relaxes.

"Have dinner with me tonight?" He smiles that panty melting smile that I can't say no to.

"Okay." I smile warmly at him knowing that we're okay even though I said no to his ridiculous proposal.

"Good. Pack a bag," he says before crushing his mouth to mine.

"I'm going blind!" Liam shouts causing both Wes and I to laugh.

chapter 9

nothing

IT'S ALWAYS WEIRD TO me how things can look more sinister in the daylight.

As kids, we're told that the bogeyman only comes out at night. That monsters hide under the bed or in the closet—but you'll never see one during the daytime.

In my profession, we see the bogeyman at all hours and monsters can be dressed as anyone.

Standing in the alleyway behind the strip club where a woman was murdered last night should be less scary today in the daylight, but right now, I feel anything but calm. There is no blood on the sidewalk, no torn clothes or bullet casings. To any other person, this would seem like any ordinary back alley, not a murder scene.

But I know differently.

I'm frozen staring at the dumpster, the backdrop of where she was found, but that's not what scares me. I feel someone watching me. I know that sounds crazy, but in my gut, someone is near and it has the hairs on my arms standing on end.

I turn and look over my shoulder but no one is there.

I look back to the dumpster where "Angel" also known as Bonnie Bradley was left—posed to be sleeping, really—as a gift. But for who? I vow to find the killer of this woman cut down in her prime—but also the reason why. There has to be a reason why someone would do something so evil.

Through my swirling thoughts and the facts of this case, all I can hear is Emma's voice saying, *"I have never seen that color on anyone other than your dad, Liam . . . and you."*

Surely, we're not the only ones in the entire tri state area with violet eyes. Bonnie is just a few years older than Liam, who was a honeymoon baby for our parents. I know it's possible that my mom and dad had lives before us, before each other, but I seriously doubt my dad would have a daughter that he didn't tell us about. My dad is all about family.

I'm so lost in my thoughts staring at this damned dumpster that I don't hear anyone approach. I barely cover the jolt that the voice behind me sends through my body. So, there is one thing to be proud of.

"No one's supposed to be back here. This is a business not a circus side show!" I turn around at his booming voice. "Oh, it's you, Detective."

"Hello, Mr. Byrd."

"Please, call me Bob," he purrs as his eyes make a slow pass down my body and the back up again, seeming to get stuck on my breasts and unable to move back up to meet my face.

I clear my throat. "Do you need something, Mr. Byrd?" The sound of my voice seems to snap him out of his fog.

"No, no," he says. "I'll just let you get to it."

"Thanks," I say as I turn back to the dumpster. I need to give this alleyway my full attention. I'm missing something but I just don't know what.

"Actually . . ." he hedges.

"Yes?" I ask.

"Do you dance?"

"What?" What in the hell is he asking me? I'm trying to find a killer and Bob Byrd is asking me if I dance. Is he asking me out? Oh hell no.

"Well, I couldn't help but notice that you have a beautiful body . . ." he trails off.

"Umm . . ." I'm not really sure how to respond here. This isn't something they cover at the Academy.

"And as of last night, I'm short a dancer. I think you would make a wonderful addition to the weekend lineup—"

"Let me stop you right there." I hold up a hand silencing him. "While I appreciate the offer, I am very busy as a police detective trying to solve the murder of the woman who had previously danced in your establishment. So, if you don't mind, I'd like to get back to that."

"Sure, sure." I again turn back to the alleyway, already having moved on from the conversation when he interrupts my thoughts again. "I was wondering if you're free for dinner tonight."

"I'm seeing someone," I say without turning back to look at him.

"Is it serious?"

"As a heart attack," I answer gravely.

"Okay, carry on." He waves his hand out magnanimously and I want to rip his arm off and beat him with that hand. I could never be a politician. Or a politician's wife. Just reason number four hundred sixty-seven why Wes's parents hate me. Oh well. Can't win them all.

"Thank you." I don't bother to turn back to him that last time either.

After a beat, I hear the back door open and close. It seems that Mr. Byrd is done waiting for me to answer him. Good. I run through the facts in my head.

Last night, after performing for a bachelor party, Bonnie Bradley was murdered and then dressed in odd clothing—old fashioned floral prints with lace collar and cuffs. Looked to be homemade. She was then laid out as if she was sleeping, as if she was a doll, but why?

Her eyes.

Something tells me that the key to why is in her eyes. I just don't know why. I walk around to the back of the dumpster. Last night, Crime Scene found scuff marks from the back door of the club to behind the dumpster. All signs leading to Bonnie being dragged back her before she was killed.

A condom wrapper was also recovered behind the dumpster. Emma will be able to tell me after she performs the autopsy if Bonnie had consensual sex with a lover before she died or if she was raped. Or maybe neither. Maybe someone had a little too much fun in the club and decided to carry it out here. What did the cab driver say? Only tricks and dancers in the club. Someone could have paid for the extra special treatment out back. Only time will tell. Until then, I have more rocks to peek under in this investigation.

There is nothing left for me here. At least not right this second, so I turn on my heel and head to my department SUV at the end of the alley. I unlock the doors with the key fob and climb in heading back towards the station.

I need to see it all laid out before me. Sometimes that helps me see the bigger picture and connect all of the dots.

I don't turn on the radio in the car, instead, I opt for silence and the company of my own thoughts, which is never good. By all accounts Bonnie Bradley was a nice woman who lived a quiet life other than when she was taking her clothes off for money. And yet, somebody wanted her dead. But who?

I pull into my usual parking spot at the station, shut the car off, and grab my folder full of notes and pictures. I let my frustration over the lack of evidence or really anything in this case show by slamming the door a little harder than I should.

I walk straight through the station and do not stop at my desk. I do not stop at the kitchenette for some coffee. I do not pass go and collect two hundred dollars. I keep walking until I reach the door to the conference room.

I slam my file down on the table and start piecing together the timeline, laid out for me to see across the table. I take each piece of evidence, each picture, each slip of paper, one by one and pin them to the bulletin board in the conference room. Hoping beyond all hope that something will click into place. Something will lead me to the who or the why or the how.

And nothing. Nothing makes sense. I beginning to think that the worst is yet to come. That after forbidding everyone to say what we were all thinking last night, that there is no refuting the fact that this case is different. That if more women turn up having been left the same way, that we have a serial killer on our hands.

I stand there with my hands on my hips staring at the board for who knows how long. It could have been minutes but my guess is it was hours. I hear a throat clear behind me and I know who it is. I'm not ready to give up and yet, I know that I need to. I need to go home and rest. I need to recharge my batteries so that I can hit the trail again tomorrow and pray to all that's holy that we don't have a psycho on our hands when I'm really afraid that we do.

"It's time to go, honey."

chapter 10

TIME TO GO.

I feel my spine straighten at Wes's softly spoken words. I look to the clock on the wall, it's a quarter past seven, the regular shift is long gone and only the night shift would be here by now.

"Lee's gone," he says as he slowly saunters my way. "You want to grab some dinner?"

"Yeah." I don't really, but I don't want to tell Wes that either. He's slowly earning his place with me. I feel guilty for having put him through his paces, but I want to believe he won't let me down.

"Let's go."

Wes helps me collect my notes and stack them in a nice, neat pile in my folder. I slide my arms into my jacket and we head out of the station. The bullpen is barren. The lights are dimmed and the chairs are tucked into their matching desks. The geriatric computers have all been put to sleep for the evening. Everyone has gone home for the night.

It feels a little like that kid book, *Goodnight Moon.* Good night papers, goodnight folders, good night battered desks and broken chairs, good night crime is everywhere.

Wes holds the glass doors in the front open for me as we both wave goodbye to the night desk sergeant, before walking silently through the parking lot with his hand on the small of my back. When we reach his car, he pulls the passenger door open for me and I climb in. We don't say a word to each other, both lost in our thoughts as he drives us towards the familiar building of comfort and family—well, not for me. Mama still holds out hope that Wes will choose her granddaughter instead of me. I find comfort in the food and the wine—and she loves Wes so much she lets me eat there, but only with him.

"Ready?" He asks me breaking into my thoughts.

I turn in my seat and look at Wes unsure of how to answer his question or the true meaning behind it. Does he mean am I ready to eat? Am I ready to find a possibly unhinged killer? Or ready to get married? Hopefully, not that one. So, I answer him the only possible way I can as I unbuckle my seatbelt and move to open my door.

"I was born ready."

We climb out of the car and head inside out of the spring chill. Mama's face immediately brightens when she sees Wes.

"Wesley! You've come to see Mama!" But then she catches a look at me holding Wes's hand and her face dims. "Oh, it's you."

She grabs menus and leads us to a table in the back.

Wes—the total shit that he is—is chuckling under his breath. I'm glad he finds this so hilarious. I mumble asshole under my breath. I know that he hears it because he only laughs louder and squeezes my hand tighter.

Wes pulls my chair out for me and Mama grumbles something about a waste before dropping menus in our laps.

"You know, I'm not sure the food is worth it," I muse as I look over the menu even though I already know what I'm getting.

"It is."

"Your opinion is invalid!" I snap and Wes just laughs.

"No, it's not."

"It is. This is all your fault anyways," I gripe.

"How is it my fault?" he asks his eyes dancing with amusement.

"She doesn't like me because she wants you to marry her granddaughter," I explain.

"So?"

"So? So, if you could get on that it would be great. Then I could eat in peace." Although the idea of Wes marrying Mama's granddaughter turns my stomach sour.

"There's only one crazy woman I want to marry and you know it. Have you thought anymore about my proposal?"

"Shh!" I panic and hide behind my menu. "Don't let anyone hear you say that!"

"Why not?" he asks.

"Because the crazy old bat with the delicious food

will throw us out without said delicious food and I'm starving!"

"I have something else in mind that I wouldn't mind eating," he says his voice husky.

"Oh no you don't!" I shout. "I'm getting linguini and you're not stopping me."

"Whatever you want, dear." Wes imitates the perfect nineteen-fifties husband. I roll my eyes as his dance with merriment.

"I like the sound of your capitulation."

"Not as much as I like the sound of yours," he says pointedly, eyes locked on mine.

"Lame. Not happening." I cross my arms over my chest.

"You know it does. Especially when you want my cock so bad that your pussy weeps and you beg me to fuck you."

"Stop. I'm losing my appetite." I say as Wes just chuckles under his breath.

After we order, I sit sipping a glass of white wine and enjoying the banter I have with Wes. I have to admit—the man gives good banter. He's sexy as hell and as we talk, laugh, and push each other's buttons, the stress of the day, of this case—of the messiness of this crime—starts to melt away. And on top of it all, Wes takes care of me too.

Our meals come and Wes and I eat in companionable silence. We're comfortable enough with each other—even after everything that's happened—that we don't need to fill the space with mindless chatter. I can't help but feel like that means something pretty significant, but I'm not ready to admit my true thoughts to myself or anyone else again.

Wes pays the check and leads me out to the car. The short drive to my apartment is quiet but the butterflies in my stomach are loud. Usually, Wes takes me back to his home instead of my small, arguably a piece of shit apartment. He hates it here. Maybe he's finally tired of me and my shit.

He parks the car and kills the engine before un-buckling his seatbelt and turning to me. I keep my eyes cast down towards my own buckle and busy my hands with that to avoid looking at Wes as he gives me the brush off. All while wondering why it was okay for me to try and scrape him off—but it hurts so bad when I know he's about to do it himself.

He gently touches his palm to my cheek and press-es his fingertips into my jaw to lift my face to meet his.

"I know what you're thinking. I can see the hamster on the wheel in there, but it's not that," he says softly.

"Okay."

"I would take you to my house, like I always do, but it's shit waking up alone after spending a great fucking night with you. Talking to you. Fucking you. Falling asleep with you in my arms. Only to then waking up to cold sheets and an empty bed." He takes a breath before continuing. "I just like being with you baby. So, since you always run here and I'm tired of chasing af-ter you in the wee hours of the morning we're staying here tonight. Even though it's a shit hole. So, wipe the sad look off of your face. It's not that."

"Okay." I can't help the wave of relief that courses through me.

"So now let's get inside so I can get inside you."

He winks—the cheeky bastard.

"Okay," I say feeling my lips twitch before climbing out of the car.

Wes rounds the hood and places his hand just above my ass on the small of my back silently letting me know that for now, he's not going anywhere. I'll take it. We walk up the steps and I let us in.

Wes softly closes the door behind us with a soft click before turning all of my locks one by one. He turns to me and I stand there watching him. Watching his surprisingly graceful movements for someone so big—so larger than life—and wondering how he decided he wanted me.

He uses the rough pads of his fingers to brush the hair that's fallen around my face back behind my ears.

"Christ, you're so beautiful," he says softly. "I could look at you forever."

"Wes—" I start but I don't get to finish my thought because his mouth crashes down on mine.

"No. No talking," he says when he lets me catch my breath. "Not tonight." Then he takes my hand and walks me back to my bedroom at the back of my apartment.

The second the door click closed behind us, Wes frames my face with his hands before touching his mouth to mine. His kiss is deep and wet and so much more. He tips his head forward when he breaks the kiss to catch his breath and his forehead touches mine. When he opens his eyes, I can tell that everything is changing between us and I'm powerless to stop it.

He skates his hands down my sides before reaching the hem of my shirt and pulling it up until it slides over my head. He reaches for the button on my jeans and pops it open before sliding the zipper down. I brush his hands away and pull his tie from around his neck. Then meticulously unbutton each button down the front of his super Fed dress shirt and then his cuffs. I slide my hands over each and every muscle on his chest and shoulders as if it's the first time I have ever touched him before letting his opened shirt slip to the floor. His belt buckle clanks as I unhook it and unzip his slacks letting them fall around his feet before pressing my palm to the prize I was searching for.

I only get to squeeze his hard length once before Wes is throwing me over his shoulder as he steps out of his shoes and pants before carrying me to the bed. Where he drops me down.

Wes slides the zipper down the side of my first boot, pulling the folded knife free and setting it on the nightstand before dropping the boot to the floor. He unzips the second boot and I get an eyebrow raised as he notices my drop gun in its holster but I just shrug. Hey, I like to be prepared for anything. He places the gun and holster on the nightstand before letting the second boot follow the first to the floor.

"Any other surprises I should know about?"

"It's always been there, I'm not sure how you've missed it." I smirk.

"We'll I guess I'll just have to frisk you then—to be sure and all," he says as he skates his hands down over my legs, gripping my ass tight in his palms before moving on and cupping my center.

"Do what you have to."

With my boots out of the way, Wes pulls my pants

down with my panties stuck inside. The look on his face is soft and his eyes blaze as he stares at me. "So fucking beautiful," he says stealing the breath from my lungs.

"Wes—"

"I'm in love with you, Claire." My eyes go wide and my mouth pops open. "I've always been in love with you. I was in love with you when you were a tiny baby in a pink blanket with bright purple eyes. It was different then. I was in love with you when you were ten years old and riding your bike to the library. I loved you before Lee and I left for the Navy. It was still different then, but still special. I was in love with you—totally gone for you—when I came home and you gave me all that was you at eighteen and it killed me to walk away. But I have always been in love with you. Now so much more than ever, baby."

"Wes—"

"You don't have to say anything now. You don't have to say it back again or as often as I do," he says wearing nothing but his underwear as he kneels between my open thighs and lays his heart at my feet. And he won't let me tell him that I love him too. He is so annoying like that.

"Wes—"

"Serious. I just needed you to know. You're so beautiful laying there, spread out like that for me. Only me."

"God damnit! Shut up." I bark and his spine goes straight. "I love you, you idiot! I have always loved you. Loved you so much it scares the shit out of me. Love you more every day. Although less right now because you were being so sweet and so romantic. I've never had that before and now you're being obnoxious not letting me get a word in." I huff out a breath.

"Are you done now?" he asks.

"Maybe. I haven't decided yet," I answer honestly.

"You're done," he says.

"You don't just get to decide that I'm done being irritated with you," I snap.

"Baby, I waited almost thirty years for you. We've been through so much. I thought I lost you twice—not in good ways—once in a really bad way. So now that I have you—in my life and in my bed—and I just told you that I have always been gone for you and you tell me that you love me but you're irritated with me. I'm going to tell you that you're over it now because my girl just gave me her heart while she's pissy. Pissy, but laying naked and fucking sexy in her bed. So I'm going to eat her and then I'm going to fuck her. Then I'm going to fuck her slow and sweet before falling asleep with her in my arms. Only to wake up with her tomorrow morning and fuck her all over again. So, you're done so I can commence that plan, okay?"

"Okay," I say stunned and definitely turned on. "You can commence your plan."

"Babe," he says as he hovers his bulky body over mine. He kisses me hard and wet and warm.

I gasp when he lets go of my mouth and trails his lips down the column of my neck, down over my collarbone, and then down to swirl around my nipple before pulling it deep into his mouth. I arch my back to give him more access as he sucks my nipple hard and then let out a whimper as he bites down on it before letting it go with a pop.

"Wes," I pant as he skims his mouth down my belly.

Wes nips my bare mound as he goes but it's not hard or mean—it's playful and tender. Before he dives in, spearing my core with his tongue as he sucks my clit into his mouth. A tingle starts at the base of my spine and I grip the sheets with my toes. I plunge my fingers into his dark hair and pull hard as he fucks me with his mouth.

I rock my pussy against his face as he shoves me over the edge into the climax that was barreling down on me full speed ahead. And I come.

Fireworks are still blasting off behind my eyes and I'm still in throws of the most magnificent climax ever to notice Wes slide his hard body up mine—divesting himself of his shorts somewhere along the way—and my pussy is still spasming when he slides his cock in deep.

My first orgasm steam rolled right into my second one as he pumps deep and hard. Faster and faster. I rake my nails down his shoulders as he chases my climax with his own, shoving his face into the crook of my neck, his lips against my skin rumbling with his groan as he comes.

When he raises his head to look at me there's a cocky smirk on his face and a twinkle in his eye. He softly touches his mouth to mine before sliding his still hard length from my body and rolling us together to his back with me laying across his chest on my belly.

Wes pulls the covers over us and tucks us in tight with my head against his chest. I hear his heart beating its steady rhythm and it pulls me into an almost deep sleep. *Almost*. But it's his words that rock me the rest of the way to dreamland.

"I've loved you your whole life and I'll love you the rest of mine." My eyes were closed and I was halfway asleep, but in the days to come I would wish that I had seen his face as he heard my returning words.

"It was only ever you, Wes. It'll only ever be you."

Then he rolled me to my back again taking my hands in each of his and holding them up by my head. I wrap my legs around his waist and hold on tight as Wes commenced the rest of his plan. Making love to me slow and sweet until a climax so bright washes over both of us that we drifted off to sleep clinging to each other.

chapter 11

someone watching

"**C**OME OUT OF THE closet, baby."

"No," I whisper, tears hot on my face and snot stuffing up my nose.

Liam and Wes were right, I'm just a baby. A big kid wouldn't be crying in the dark corner of a closet hoping it'll all go away if you just wish hard enough. I bet Wes never cries. I know Lee doesn't.

"Come out now, Claire. Playtime is over."

"No," I cry louder. "Please don't make me."

"Now!" He growls as the closet door rattles. I gasp.

"Leave me alone!"

"Get out of the fucking closet, Claire!" He roars.

"Please no," I cry harder, my body shaking with each sob.

"When," he kicks his hard boots against the closet door and it shudders.

"Please."

"Are you," he kicks it again.

The doors are the kind with the slats that fold sideways. We have them at home and mama says I always pinch my fingers in the accordion. Whatever that is.

"I just wanna go home," I whisper.

"Gonna," he kicks again.

"I just want my mommy," I sob. "Please, I just want my mommy."

"Fucking," the boards snaps and I scream.

"I just wanna go home, please," I beg.

"Learn!" he shouts as he kicks the broken boards out of the way. He leans down and grabs me by my upper arms.

"Please," I wheeze but my words are cut short when he slaps my face hard. So hard I taste blood in my mouth and it's so yucky I feel sick. I'm going to throw up from the yucky taste. I try as hard as I can not to. I know that if I do, he'll punish me again. I don't want that. Anything but that.

"You are home, baby," he coos right before he slaps me again. I cry out again, falling to the floor with his last hit. It's so strong he knocks me down with it. "And I thought I told you to call me daddy," he says as he lands a hard kick to my back.

"You're not my daddy, you'll never be my daddy," I whisper. "My daddy is a nice man. He would never hurt me. You'll never be my daddy," I say again but the bad man can't hear me, he already walked away. I have nowhere to go, but one thing is for sure, I have to escape.

I have that creepy feeling you get when you know that someone is watching. It's a feeling that has saved my life a handful of times so I snap my eyes open and see Wes is laying on his side. He's propped up on his elbow, with his head resting on his hand and his warm eyes on me.

"Hey," I rasp hoping he didn't realize that I was gripped in another nightmare.

"Morning, baby." I swallow to try and clear the sleep from my throat and open my mouth to speak but Wes beats me to it by dropping his mouth to mine. I open mine underneath his when he licks at the seam of my lips and he deepens the kiss as he rolls over my body.

"We have to get up."

"Not yet," he hums against my mouth as he slides his knees between my thighs spreading them open to his invasion of the very best kind.

"We have to go to work."

"Not yet," he murmurs as he trails his fingers down my hip and over my mound and down further. "Always so wet." He swirls his index finger around my clit making me whimper into his mouth.

"Wes—"

"Not yet," he says as he removes his finger from my clit, only to guide the tip of his cock into my wetness. I arch my back to try and take him deeper. "Not yet."

"Please, Wes." And that was all he needed to slide all the way to the root.

Wes takes my hands in his and intertwines our fingers in an intimate move that I both love and hate. I love it because it makes us so close—nose to nose—and other more fun parts. And I hate it because it's so intimate—that scares the hell out of me.

He places our joined hands up on either side of my head and as he looks into my eyes, his nose brushing mine. Wes rocks his hips softly into mine. There is no restlessness, no rush this time. Wes is not a man in a hurry, but he is a man with a desire to make love to his woman. You can see it in his eyes as he slowly puts his mouth on mine and takes us both over the edge.

When our breathing slows and the sweat on our bodies begins to cool, Wes finally looks at me and says, "Now we have to get up and get ready for work." I just roll my eyes and he laughs.

Wes pulls me up and out of bed and leads me down the hall to my small bathroom where he lifts me up by the waist and sets me on the small, soapstone countertop. He pulls the glass door open and cranks the water up. I live in a piece of shit apartment so even though the apartment is small, it takes awhile to heat up the water. So, Wes saunters back to me gloriously naked and then pushes his hips between my legs as I sit on the counter and kisses me. He doesn't just kiss me, no, Wes lazily makes out with me in his arms while we wait for the shower to heat up.

Then he plucks me from the countertop and walks straight into the shower with me in his arms. I turn into the water to wash my hair. I tip my head back under the spray to rinse the suds from my hair. Before I have a chance to stand back up I'm hauled out of the water and up against a very hard Wes.

"Do you know what you do to me, baby?" he asks.

I have an idea because it is also very hard and pressed against my belly.

"I'm starting to figure it out." I grip his hard length in my fist and pump him once, twice, before I find my front pressed against the shower wall.

"Be careful, baby. You're playing with fire." He presses in close against my back and I feel the heat of him against my ass.

"Maybe I like the risk."

He growls low in his throat before tipping my hips back and thrusting his cock deep. Wes keeps me pinned to the shower wall with his chest pressed to my back. The cool material of the shower wall at my breasts and the heat of his body at my back does things to me.

Wes sets a fast tempo of push and pull that won't keep us going long. My cheek is against the wall and I whimper. I'm so close and I want it, but Wes is even closer.

"Touch yourself, baby. Get there." Wes takes my hand from the wall in his and slides it down the wall to between my legs where his uses my finger to circle my clit and push me closer. He skates our hands deeper to where his cock moves hard and fast in and out of my body. "Feel that. This is us when you end and I begin and this is only ever going to be us. No one else." He pumps faster and faster.

"Wes—"

"Get there," he says as he moves our hands back up to circle my clit. I whimper and cry out because I'm there. He lets go of my hand and I take over as he grips my hips and thrusts harder. "Yes. you're there." And I am. I press my cheek harder to the shower wall as my finger circles my clit. Wes pushes into my body and pulls back one out, once, twice more, and then I come. Wes follows me over the edge calling out my name as he does.

As he comes back down to earth, he slowly glides his cock in and out before kissing my shoulder gently and then slipping free from my body. I lean all of my weight against the shower wall. I think I'm dead. I must have died just now but what a way to go.

I hear Wes swallow down a chuckle from behind me and then his soapy hands roam all over my body. He rains kisses down all over my shoulders and the back of my neck as he soaps up my body and his before rinsing us clean.

He shuts off the water and towels me dry before drying himself. Then we both dress for work—including my stuffing my drop gun and holster back in my boot. All while Wes watches with a twinkle of amusement in his eyes.

chapter 12

this changes everything

"**B**ABE, YOU NEED COFFEE."

"That is no lie," I share as Wes diverts from his path to the station to our favorite coffee shop. It's my favorite because the coffee is to die for. It's Wes's favorite because there is a twenty-year-old barista who fawns all over him but in an adorable—totally shy—way, so I can't even be mad at her.

Wes pulls into the parking lot as a front space magically opens. As is the way for all things where Wes is concerned. He's always been the golden boy that great things just happen to. Liam as well. Honestly, it's exhausting.

I hop out of the car intent on a caffeine infusion with Wes hot on my heels. He wraps his arm around my waist and I stiffen. I'm not used to anyone holding me while I'm wearing my duty rig. I force my muscles to relax one by one. This love and couple business is hard.

Wes pulls open the door to the coffee shop for me

and the bell over it chimes. We walk in and are greeted by Tammy the ever shy, ever adorable barista. She smiles at me like she smiles at everyone because she's just that sweet. But when she sees Wes she positively glows. Her crush is still in full swing and I love it. It's adorable in its harmless young girl to woman way. She's growing into herself and she's got a good eye, Wes is a catch. He's just my catch.

"Hello, Detective, the usual?"

"Yes, please!" I smile as she writes my name on the paper cup and hands it to the other kid to make my fancy ass coffee.

"And the usual, Sir?" she asks Wes. "A large black coffee." She knows his order by heart. It's not a hard one, but still . . .

"Yeah, Tammy. Thanks." She physically brightens at the use of her name which we both know because we come here so often. Not to mention it's on a name tag on the front of her apron.

"Coming right up. It'll be nine dollars and eighty-five cents." He glares at me as he hands her a twenty.

"Hey, these fancy coffees aren't cheap but they make me so happy." I smile sweetly at Wes.

"Keep the change," Wes adds when Tammy tries to hand him back his change.

"Oh, thank you, Sir." She breathes. I barely keep from rolling my eyes. That's a new one, the Sir bit. I wonder if she's been watching those Fifty Shades movies. She's not going to find her dom in my overly dominate guy, that's for sure. He's mine. Well, it seems a couple rounds of ridiculously good sex make me down right possessive. Who knew?

We collect our coffees and head out the door. Both climbing into the car when Wes beeps the locks with the key fob.

"Not one word," he rumbles.

"I wasn't going to say anything."

"Lord love a liar."

"I have no idea what you're talking about. Drive me to the station, Jeeves!" I laugh, then I sit back and drink my fancy ass coffee with a smile on my face as Wes drives me to the station.

He pulls into the lot and parks the car, finding another ridiculously good space. I do roll my eyes at that and catch the flash of white teeth as he smiles. We climb out of the car and walk towards the station. This time Wes does not hold me close because he knows how important it is to me to be treated with respect here—respect that I have earned with hard work and determination.

He does open the door for me and I walk through it with him on my heels.

"Goody, Emma called and the autopsy on the dancer is done," another detective calls out when I enter the bullpen.

"Thanks." I'll head down to the basement after I check in at my desk.

"I'm going to go check in with Lee. If I don't see you before I head to my office I'll see you tonight."

"Okay," I say distracted my mind already turning to what Emma has for me. Wes just shakes his head with a smile and heads down the hall towards Liam's office.

I walk straight to my desk and sit down, placing

my paper coffee cup on the desk in order to boot up my geriatric computer. Once that task is done I notice a huge pile of mail on my desk and sigh. It's only seven in the morning, how can I possibly have so much mail?

The biggest is on top. It's a giant manila envelope with no postage or address on it. Just my name typed out on the front. Someone must have dropped this off in person. I flick back the little metal clip that holds it closed and pull out the stack of papers neatly tucked inside. On top is a typed note.

Do you know what your boyfriend is doing when you're not looking?

That's all that the note said. That's all that was typed on one white sheet of printer paper. The hair on the back of my neck stands on end. It's an omen of things to come—and not a good one. I flip the note over, face down next to the stack and am greeting with a series of glossy eight by tens. Enough to burst the happy love bubble that I was in with Wes and leave nothing but shrapnel and carnage.

What. The. Fuck.

When I had sat down at my desk and opened the manila envelope that was left on top of my stack of mail. It had seemed harmless enough.

But it wasn't.

I blink my eyes over and over trying to make my brain process what it's seeing but I can't. I can't unsee the images from the stack of pictures in my hand. Giant glossy eight by tens from different angles. So there is absolutely no doubt that my heart is breaking.

And it is broken. It's not just broken it's *shattered.*

"It's not what it looks like," I hear from over my

shoulder and I have to grit my teeth to keep from screaming.

I shuffle the pictures sliding the top one to the back of the stack so that I can see the next in line. This one is zoomed in. His head is tipped back and his face is distorted with both lust and passion as she straddles his lap. Her hands hold his to her breasts and I can see the play of tendons flex through them as he grips them tight. It was only two nights ago that his hands were on my own breasts much the same way as I rode his cock on the sofa.

"Claire, did you hear me?" he asks but I shuffle the stack again. In this picture, he has his arms wrapped around her back and he's pulling her close—her breasts mashed up against his strong chest. Her hands with long, red painted talons press in on either side of his face and as they kiss hungrily, their mouths open as their tongues tangle. "God damnit, Claire! Did you hear me?" My spine turns to steel.

"I did. I'm just choosing to ignore you."

"Don't do this, baby," he growls.

"I'm not the one who did anything."

"I can explain." But I'm not interested in listening to him plead a case when he is more than guilty.

"I'm going to need you to leave, Wes."

"No."

"This changes everything."

"This changes nothing! Fuck that, Claire," he yells. "You want to run away. You have *always* wanted to run away. And here is your fucking reason to served up on a goddamn silver platter."

"No," I shout back as I throw the stack of glossy

betrayal down on top of my desk as I push my rolly chair back and stand. It slams into the desk behind mine. "You do not get to come in here, where I work, and tell me that I am to blame for your bullshit."

"Okay," he says as he holds his hands up in surrender. "You're right. I'm sorry. I can see you need time."

"I need a lot of things. One of them is definitely distance."

"I don't know if I can give you that. I can't lose you, baby." His words burn hot behind my eyes and the last thing I want is for the other guys in the bullpen to see me cry.

"You should have thought about that before you fooled around with that stripper."

"Claire—" he starts but I don't let him finish.

"You need to go now," I say softly.

I stand with my feet apart, my hands on my hips, and my head bowed as if I'm waiting for a blow. He looks at me and opens his mouth as if he's going to try to explain again. Something in my stance must have told him it was a losing battle because he snaps his mouth closed before moving towards the exit.

Wes pauses just before opening the door to turn and look back at me. I see him in my peripheral, but I'm looking at his lies and deceit spread across my desk for all to see. He pulls open the door and then slams it on his way out. This is definitely how my heart breaks.

"You okay?" I hear from over my shoulder. I'm not in the mood to deal with anyone right now. I need to be alone to sort my feelings. I need to be alone to sort this fucking case.

"Yeah, I just need to get down to the morgue." I

shrug. "Duty calls."

"You sure about?" I look up at Cruz and his face is so open and honest—something I have not had a lot of in my life—that I feel compelled to answer him when he asks again. "Are you going to be alright?"

"I'm not sure I even know the answer to that."

"Then he didn't deserve you to begin with." I'm not sure how to respond to that. At all. "I'm here if you need me."

"Duty calls," I say again and head to the elevator that will take me to the basement. The doors open and I step inside. Just as they're about to close Cruz is there with a hand to the door.

"Just think about what I said." And then he lets go of the door and the elevator takes me to Emma's lair in the basement.

chapter 13

windows to the soul

"**S**TEP RIGHT UP, LADIES and gentlemen. We have a winner! Whaaaa," Emma shouts in her best game show host voice as I step off the elevator.

"And they think I'm the one who needs the department shrink." I shrug.

"That's because you do." She winks at me to lessen the sting of what we both know to be the truth.

"Thank you." I roll my eyes.

"Because you're a lunatic. Totally batty. Mad. Bonkers," Emma says in her best impression of the Mad Hatter.

"Takes one to know one." I stick out my tongue which only makes Emma cackle. I'm really mature, I know.

"'Only the best people are,'" she says finishing the *Alice in Wonderland* quote.

"Am I down here in your evil lair for a reason?" I change the subject.

"You are!" she cheers brightly.

"And that would be?" I'm a little shorter than I usually am with her and it makes her tip her head to the side to study me.

"Is everything okay, Claire?" She asks.

I sigh. "Just peachy."

"Claire," she whispers. "No."

"It's fine . . . I'll be fine."

"Is Liam okay?" Now it's my turn to study her.

"Why wouldn't he be?"

"No reason," she hedges.

"Is it Anna?" she asks.

"No."

"Wes?" she asks with her hand to her chest.

"Cheated. He's a filthy fucking liar."

"You don't know that for sure," she says after a pregnant pause.

"I have a stack of pictures on my desk that say otherwise, doll," I say softly.

"Oh no."

"Yeah." I sigh again. There's a band around my chest that keeps getting tighter and tighter and there's nothing I can do to ease the tension. Maybe I'm having a heart attack.

"Do you want me to call Anna?" she asks. That's my Emma, always ready to rally the troops in an emergency. But Wes isn't going to be an emergency. He was the slow-motion car crash I saw coming from miles away.

"No." I take a deep breath. "So, what do you have for me?"

"Maybe we shouldn't do this now."

"Why not?" I ask.

"I had to let Liam know I needed him for this. Maybe you don't want to see him right now."

"What?" I jump. "Why would you call Lee?"

"Why wouldn't she?" he barks from behind me. "I'm the fucking Captain, *Detective*," he says reminding me of my place here at the station while dressing me down at the same time.

"Because you were there the night the homicide took place."

"We don't know that it's a homicide yet," he snaps making me wonder if mom dropped him on his head as a baby.

"Don't be dumb, Liam."

"I'm just saying . . ." He holds his hands up at his sides in a *so what* gesture.

"Actually, we do know that she was murdered." Emma interjects.

"What do you have?" I ask.

"She had enough benzene in her bloodstream to immobilize her pretty quickly."

"How quick?" Lee asks.

"Maybe a minute or two."

"What's benzene?" I ask.

"It's a chemical—man made—that can be found in everything from drycleaners to gasoline."

"So, our guy is a dry cleaner?" Lee asks.

"Your guy can be anything, *El Capitan*," Emma snaps at him obviously losing her patience. "You can Prime that shit and have it delivered to your doorstep in two days."

"Fuck." Lee bites out.

"How did he give it to her?" I ask.

"Here." Emma peels back the sheet showing us the victim from the shoulders up pointing to a tiny little dot in between her neck and shoulder that I never would have noticed. "He injected it here."

"So, the killer poisoned her."

"No," Emma tells Liam and I like were the slow class. "He *immobilized* her first. Then the other stuff."

"Start at the beginning," Lee barks.

"My guess would be he lured her out back or found her there. Once the benzene was in her body, she would have dropped quickly. She would be like an over cooked noodle. He could have undressed her then—"

"She was already naked," Liam says quietly. "She was the dancer at Jones's party."

"Then she was raped," Emma says filling in the gaps.

"DNA?" I ask getting excited for a lead.

"No. Vaginal tearing and condom lubricant were all that was present."

"God damnit!" Lee bites out.

"Then how did she die?" I ask.

"He strangled her." She takes a deep breath before continuing. "She would have had to be dressed and posed quickly before rigor set in."

"Jesus." He rubs a heavy palm down his face.

"Okay," I say hesitantly. "This case is weird. But why did you need Lee here?"

She looks at me hard. "Are you sure you want to do this right now?"

"Emma," I warn.

"What am I missing?" Liam asks.

"She caught Wes cheating," Emma says bluntly.

"What?" Lee shouts. "I'll kill him. But when? With who?"

"With whom, you mean," Emma corrects.

"With her." I point to the dead stripper. Liam starts laughing. "What's so funny?" I snap.

"Nothing. Nothing at all. But Wes didn't cheat." Liam says, still laughing.

"I have a stack of pictures on my desk that say otherwise."

"I was with him all night. She danced for most of us, Claire."

"Even lap dances?" Now he looks at me like I'm the stupid one.

"Yeah, sis, it was a bachelor party. Either her or her friend rubbed their body glitter off on everyone in the group."

"Even kissing?" He laughs harder. "Stop that!"

"Honey, that's part of their thing," he explains gently.

"You made out with her the other night?" Emma asks from the corner sounding a mix of disgusted and disappointed.

"No." He shrugs. "Her friend. Actually, I was going to get a little more from her, but your boy needed a smoke and there this one was."

"He didn't cheat?" I ask. Lee's face softens and his laughter cuts off.

"No, honey. He loves you," my brother says softly, reverently as if I somehow stumbled onto the holy grail.

"Fuck!" I shout.

"What?" Lee asks.

"Fuck, fuck, fuck!"

"What?" Lee repeats his earlier question.

"She broke up with him," Emma drolls.

"I didn't break up with him . . . *per se*. I said I needed time and distance. But the note made it sound like he's been cheating all along."

"What note?" they both shout in unison.

"The note that came with the pictures."

"I think you were set up, sis. I need to see that package." We turn to head towards the elevator to get to the bottom of this whole Wes cheater drama when Emma stops us in our tracks.

"Wait!"

"What?" we say together.

"You haven't heard it all. Why Lee needed to be her too. It's not because it's your case," she says before pulling the rug out from under Lee and me. "It's because it's personal."

"How is it personal?" I ask. "Lee didn't kiss her and Wes didn't cheat."

"Remember I said her eyes were unusual? Windows to the soul they are," Emma explains.

"Yeah . . ." I reply hesitantly.

"That I had only ever seen eyes like that on you, Lee, and your dad," she continues.

"Yes." I enunciate the word.

"That color is rare. You don't see it often. And I was right, she doesn't wear contacts. So I tested her DNA . . ."

"And?" Lee snaps.

"She was your sister."

chapter 14

bad at love

I STEP INTO THE coffee shop. It's familiar but not because I get my coffee here. It's familiar because she works here.

Her black hair is driving me mad. I have to have it. It's dark and shiny but not glossy like a raven's wing and that makes me angry. Because this she is not the one that I want—the one that I need. No, she won't fucking notice me. I showed her how awful he is, how he doesn't deserve her, but does she choose me? No!

This one wants him too. I can see it the way she smiles at him when he comes here for coffee. She's practically begging him to want her. I feel the same way for the other one. The one I want but I won't beg her to love me. She will. I'll make sure of it.

But until then . . .

"Can you help me?" I ask sneaking up on this one as she stocks some shelves in the back all alone.

"Oh! I'm sorry, you startled me."

"You're lovely," I say to her.

"What?" she asks surprised as the tip of my needle slides into her pale skin of her neck.

"I said 'you're absolutely lovely.'" I tell her as I drop her to the storeroom floor and reach back to lock the door. "Almost perfect."

She looks at me with judgement in her eyes.

"This isn't for you to judge or decide," I seethe. "This is for me. I need her."

I look at her clear blue eyes and they're all wrong. Her eyes aren't purple. All. Wrong. Allwrongallwrongallwrongalwrong.

I strip her of her hideous clothes—she'll be perfect when I'm done with her. Like a little porcelain doll.

I might have given her too much of the benzene. Even her eyelids don't move.

Well, better get to it.

The condom wrapper crinkling is the only sound around. I roll the rubber down my length thinking of hair as glossy as a raven's wing and then I pull gloves onto my hands before wrapping them around her slim neck which is not as graceful as a dancer's, not like hers. And then I squeeze.

"Absolutely lovely," I lie.

"What?" Liam asks softly.

"I compared her DNA with Claire's sample from her file. Bonnie Bradley, age forty-three, is your sister—well, half-sister."

"That doesn't make any sense," I say. "That means—"

"Dad had another life before mom," Lee adds. "Don't you remember, I was their honeymoon surprise? They weren't even married a year when I was born and I'm thirty-eight."

"Okay," I sigh as the truth sinks in. "Dad didn't—"

"No," he says. "But it does mean we just lost a sister we didn't know we had."

"Now, I'm super glad she's not the one you kissed," Emma adds. "But it does make it weird that your boyfriend kissed your sister." She points at me. This is very true. My life is not a fun place to be right now.

"This is also true," Lee says looking at Emma like he's seeing her for the first time. Oh hell, this is going to blow up in our faces. Wes and I are bad at love, but Lee and either of my two friends that have feelings for him—or both, can anyone say *love triangle*—is a bad fucking idea.

"Lee—" I start but I'm interrupted by the ringing of my phone.

"Goodnite," I answer.

"Detective Goodnite, this is dispatch."

"Go ahead, Dispatch."

"We have officers responded to a homicide at a coffee shop. Case details are . . . similar to yours. They advised we notify you."

"Send me the address, I'm on my way," I say before ending the call.

"What's up?" Liam asks, suddenly alert.

"Got a fresh one."

"Another body?" He asks.

"Yep."

"Oooh, ooh, ooh. Pick me!" Emma jumps up and

down.

"Yes, Em?" I ask.

"Is it as creepy as the last one?" She just can't help herself. We all know that these are real people who have been victimized, some even murdered. But in our line of work if we don't find some kind of levity in all of the seediness and evil, we'll crack.

"I don't know yet as I am not there—I am here. So, I gotta go." I look at my phone, the address of the restaurant when my body is. "Oh, fuck."

"What?" they both shout again.

"It's our coffeeshop," I explain.

"What?"

"The one that Wes and I always go to that costs a ton but I love it. So, we go and there is an adorable college girl that is over the moon for Wes. It's fucking adorable and she's so sweet." I make a strangled noise before bolting for the door to the stairs. There's no time for the elevator.

"Claire!" Lee screams.

"Fuck! Lee, she was on shift this morning. I have to go."

"I'm right behind you!" he shouts following me out.

If someone had asked me, I wouldn't be able to tell them how I got here. I ran up the stairs and out of the morgue. I know that I must have jumped in my department truck, but that's it. Between the phone call from dispatch and now—looking at Tammy's body laid out like a God damned doll—I couldn't tell you how I got from there to here.

Tammy Campbell, a nineteen-year-old college coed who this morning had the whole world laid out before her, now lays on her side in a dress that looks like it belongs in a production of *Our Town*. Her black hair is fanned out around her and her eyes are closed. Her hands are up in prayer, forever dreaming under her cheek—like a *fucking doll*.

I can already see the purple bruises coming up on her neck.

"Claire," Wes says from behind me, his voice pained. But of course, it would be. This is Tammy. *Our Tammy*. The girl we always buy coffee from. The girl who harmlessly flirts with Wes every single time.

But maybe it wasn't so harmless.

"This is an active crime scene, Agent O'Connell," I clip.

"Claire?" he asks. He sounds confused. "Lee called and said I needed to come here. He said you needed me."

"I need to solve this case and to do that I need you not here." I take a deep breath.

"You don't mean that," he pleads.

"I do, Wes. I have to figure this out before more people die."

"Claire—" he starts but I don't let him finish.

"You have to go. Someone else you were near died and I have to find out why."

"That's not fucking fair!" he yells, his hips and his feet wide.

"But it's true."

"You can't possibly think I did this." His tone is incredulous. Wes is mad, maybe a little hurt, I don't know. All I know is that I have to figure this shit out before it gets any worse.

"I don't know what to think anymore, Wes. But the signs are pointing to this being about you and you know it. Angel danced for you, kissed you. She's dead. The whole world knew Tammy had a mammoth sized crush on you and now she's dead too. Who's next, Wes?" I ask. It's an unfair question and we both know it but I ask it anyways.

"Low blow, Goodnite," he clips out. Wes's entire body is perfectly still as a statue but his eyes, his eyes are wild.

"Someone has to ask the question. Now if you'll excuse me, I'll get back to doing just that."

"You have to talk to me, Claire. We have to talk about this."

"Don't leave town," I say as I move around another officer and make my way away from Wes.

chapter 15

old news

ISTAND IN THE hallway of the small coffee shop that I will never be a patron of again and watch the hustle a bustle of the Crime Scene Unit. Cameras flash and bootied feet shuffle as people poke and prod Tammy Campbell in the last place she was ever vibrant and alive.

I stand as a silent sentry guarding her in her last moments before she heads to Emma's lair in the morgue, giving her these last vestiges of dignity and privacy. With my hands on my hips and my feet shoulder width apart, I watch as the team loaded her onto a gurney and then rolled out the back doors into the alley to load her into the back of the Medical Examiner's body mover van. And through it all I can't help but think that her hair is black just like mine.

When the heavy metal doors slam closed behind her I turn on my heels and get back to work. I notice Liam and Wes are standing there—eyes locked on my every move like heat seeking missiles. That's fine. They won't bother me. I'm in my zone, this is my world and they just get to play in it. I will find out what happened to Tammy and Bonnie no matter the cost—even if the high price is my affair with Wes.

I walk back inside the shop and another girl is hysterical. She's sobbing so hard she can't catch her breath. She's sitting at a table with a woman of middle age with some slight silvering to her hair. She's the manager, I've met her before.

"Can I sit down and talk to you guys for a bit?" I ask.

The older woman looks to the younger one in her arms. The young barista nods. So, does the manager.

"Thank you," I say softly. "Were you both working this morning?"

"I was," the manager tells me.

"No." The girl sniffles.

"Who found her?" I ask.

"I did," the young woman says before biting her lip to hold in a wail. "I had just clocked in and Maggie told me to find out what Tammy was up to."

"Where were you?" I asked the manager.

"I was in the office doing payroll. I hate math. I do it when the store is slow between rush hour and lunch."

"That's understandable." I smile sweetly.

"Thank you."

"Were either of you close with Tammy?"

"Of course," the manager says. "My girls are like daughters to me."

"That's true," the younger woman agrees. "Tammy is . . . *was* my best friend," she chokes out.

"Would you say you knew her well?" I ask.

"Yes," she answers immediately.

"Was she seeing anyone?"

"Sh-she was umm," she clears her throat. Her eyes are searching wildly around the room, she's looking anywhere but at me.

"Whatever you have to say is okay. You're not in any trouble," I reassure her. I can see that she's afraid to hit me with some old news.

"She was in love with your boyfriend. She was hoping he would take notice of her one day. Tammy said she had a plan to make that happen." Apparently, Tammy wasn't as cute and sweet as I had originally thought. And instantly I feel bad for thinking ill of the dead.

"So, she wasn't seeing anyone?"

"No," she whispers. It appears that I'm not the only one who was in love with Wes. This is really getting old.

chapter 16

crash and cry

IT'S BEEN A LONG fucking day.

When I finish up with the manager and the barista it's late into the afternoon and I know that I can't take anymore. I need booze and food. I need to cry and to crash. In that order.

So, I head out. I toss a hand up in a wave to the officers left at the scene that I recognize and head out to my truck and fire her up. It's days like these that I wish my favorite Chinese restaurant that delivered wasn't ruined for me—for all time—by an idiotic asshole who was lead around by his dick by a murderous psychopath. I mentally shrug off that negativity as I remember I found a new place that's decent.

I could really go for some Chinese right now. But the thought of fried rice or even my favorite mu-shu chicken has my stomach turning sour. That could also be because the last time I ate there the murderous psycho duet tried to poison me so that's out.

I'll just get a pie. Pizza is always good.

I pick my phone up out of the cup holder where I always put it while I'm driving to call my favorite place for delivery so that it gets there the same time I do when my phone rings.

"Hello?" I answer.

"I heard you had a rough day, Claire. Do you need to talk?" Anna asks.

"Hey, Anna. I'm alright."

"Are you sure?"

"Yes." I sigh. "Maybe."

"Are you going home to binge on pizza, bourbon, and old episodes of the Real Housewives?"

"Are you spying on me?" I ask. "It's like you're in my brain."

She laughs. "No, silly. That's the girl solution to heartbreak and a bad case rolled into one."

"You sound like you're acutely familiar with this particular brand of medicine . . ." I bait.

"Nah, I'm a tough chick. The dating prospects are just worse than usual this month," she says after a long pause.

"This is a really shitty case," I say, my mood taking a turn for the worse.

"They do seem to be pretty personal lately," she agrees.

"Yeah. That they do."

"Okay, so, girls' night?" she asks. "Pedis, facials, and enough Ben & Jerry's and Wild Turkey to kill a herd of elephants. And of course, Emma and I."

"I appreciate it, I do. But I just don't think I'm up to it tonight," I explain as I pull into my usual spot at my apartment complex and my thoughts shifting to last night in Wes's arms as he told me that he loved me.

"*Which is exactly why we should do it tonight.*" She rallies as I climb the steps to my front door.

"Look, I just got home," I tell her. "I promise not to drink a whole bottle of Wild Turkey and then drown myself in the bathtub over a lousy man." I let myself into my apartment. There's a box that looks like it's flowers on the kitchen counter. Wes was here.

"*One, that's not funny and two, you don't have a bathtub,*" Anna chastises me.

"See? Exactly! I'm safe to order a pizza and just be. Look I have to deal with Wes's lame attempt to garner my forgiveness and find something to put in my belly to soak up all the booze I'm planning to drink." Truth be told, I just need to be alone in the quiet with my thoughts.

"*Ooooh, what did he do now?*" she asks.

"It looks like he dropped off flowers as an apology," I explain. "I gotta go."

"*Okay, but keep me posted!*" she says before she rings off.

I set my phone down on the kitchen counter and reach for the big red bow on the box to untie it. I can't help myself, I have to see what Wes sent even though I know that I should just throw it into the garbage. I pull the white cardboard top off of the long, rectangular box and see what has to be at least two or three dozen—maybe even four dozen—of the most gorgeous blood red, long-stemmed roses.

I dig my fingers through the stems careful of the thorns but find no card. Weird. But then again, why would Wes send a card? I know it's him. I just thought that maybe he would, I don't know, explain, or tell me how much he loves me, apologize even. But then again, men are stupid. I should be the bigger person and call him to thank him for the flowers.

I pick up my phone off the counter and turn my back to the box of flowers on the kitchen counter while I listen to his phone ring and ring. I'm just about to give up when he answers.

"Claire."

"Hey, yeah . . . umm . . . it's me," I say feeling as awkward as I sound. Maybe even worse.

"I know who you are, baby," his deep voice rumbles over the line.

"Okay, yeah, well. I just wanted to say thank you for the flowers." But I'm met with silence on the other end. "Wes?"

"Honey," he says hesitantly. *"I didn't send you any flowers."*

"No, the ones you left in my kitchen on the counter. Don't play games, Wes. Who else would leave flowers in my apartment for me."

"Claire," he says and there is something in his tone that makes my back go ramrod straight and stop everything. *"I didn't leave you any flowers either. Get out of there."*

"What?" I say as I turn around to face the box of flowers on my countertops. I see something flash.

"Claire—"

"There's something in the box."

"Claire, get out of there—" but I don't hear the rest of what he was saying because like a flash of lightning something jumped out and struck my forearm.

I let out a blood curdling scream worthy of any dumb chick in a scary movie.

"Claire! What's happening?" Wes shouts.

"R-r-r-rattlesnake," I say as I hear the *ch-ch-chhh* of its warning rattle *after* it strikes. And then everything goes black.

I watch her as she races home to find my gift and it's even better than I could have anticipated. She has absolutely no idea!

When I saw the flowers in the florist's window, I knew she had to have them. Everyone knows that red roses signify admiration or devotion but that a deep red rose, can mean regret and sorrow. These were absolutely perfect for the message that I wanted to send her. How much I long for her, how much I want her, how devoted I am to her. But the regret and sorrow for killing. I shouldn't have to kill the imperfect, I should be with her. Yes, the blood red roses were the perfect message to send.

And so was the snake.

I am angry with her. How hard should I have to work to show her that she belongs to me? I am her everything and she can't even see it! She needs to learn her lessons. To take what is being offered to her and leave the Fed in the dust or else there will be conse-quences. Grave consequences.

I hear her scream as she finds her other present and the sound has me rock hard. I unzip my jeans and pull out my cock. I stroke myself thinking of hair the color of a raven's wing and eyes like bright amethysts, but it's the sound of her scream repeating in my head that has me coming in my fist.

chapter 17

"**W**ES?"

"I'm right here, honey." I hear a beeping and look around. I'm in a hospital room. The scratchy sheets and blankets abrade my legs.

"Wh-what happened?" I ask. My voice sounds timid and weak. Young. I sound so young and helpless and I hate it.

"You were bit by a rattlesnake." I tip my head to the side to look at him. Is he joking? "There was no poison in your body so it was either a baby and you got fucking lucky or it had had its venom removed which is creepy as hell. But also makes you lucky and also makes you not lucky because you've caught the attention of a lunatic. I have to tell you I do not have good feelings about that."

"A rattlesnake?" I ask.

"Yes."

"Where would I have found a rattlesnake . . ." I trail off before the memories come crashing back into my head. "The roses."

"Yeah, honey," Wes says and his voice is grim.

"You didn't send them." It's not a question that I have asked. We both know something nefarious is happening here.

"No, baby."

"Someone sent me flowers with a rattlesnake."

"Yes."

"Someone put flowers with a rattlesnake in my apartment," I say and my panic is audible.

"Yes—" he starts. I can tell that Wes is going to try and placate me.

"Someone was in my house."

"Yes—"

"Someone was in my house!" I shriek.

"Claire."

"Someone was in my house!" I scurry back in the hospital bed afraid and I hate that. I hate that some monster in the dark has made me afraid and that makes me fucking angry.

"Claire, baby."

"Someone was in my fucking house!" "I need help in here!" he shouts as he jumps up from his chair and is rounding my hospital bed but I continue to scoot back. I can't trust anyone. I don't even know if I can trust Wes. And that is the scariest part of the whole shit sandwich that has become my life.

"Don't come any closer." He freezes.

"Claire, honey. You can't mean that," Wes says. His voice is full of hurt and regret.

"Someone went into my apartment and left me a box of gorgeous roses that contained a rattlesnake,

Wes. I mean everything." I pant. I can't seem to take a deep enough breath. I'm losing my cool. I'm panicking. I feel like the walls are closing in and the room is spinning. I can't catch my breath. I can't breathe as spots dance before my eyes.

"Claire, baby. You're scaring me." And then someone turns out the lights. "Claire?" he calls out but it sounds like he's far away. Like he's at the far end of a tunnel or under water. Maybe I'm the one who is underwater because it feels like I'm sinking down, down, down, so very deep down. Why is Wes so very far away?

Just as the world goes black I hear, "I need some help! She's crashing!"

I love him.

I love Wes. He's so handsome and so grown up. He's got dark hair with just a little wave to it and light brown eyes. But best of all he's nice to me.

Today Wes and Liam promised mama that they would be here for supper. I love when we all hang out together. The boys don't stay here very often anymore. They say they're going into the Navy, whatever that means, and I won't see them anymore. I don't like that.

The doorbell rings before it opens. That's weird, Wes never rings the bell. He's family. Always has been, daddy says. Wes walks through the door with two girls. This is terrible. Two grownup girls with makeup and boobies.

Liam meets them in the entryway and kisses the one

with dark hair. Wes has his arm wrapped around the one with yellow hair and I hate her.

Tears start rolling down my cheeks and I wipe them away with my hands. I hate crying. Liam and daddy always told me to be tough so I don't cry much. I turn on my heels and run to my room and climb under my blankets.

I don't know how long I lay there deep in my blankets, all I know is that I finally stopped crying when there's a knock at my door.

"Go away," I say just loud enough.

"Can't do that squirt," Wes says as he peers around my door. "My girl isn't at dinner and I miss her." His words hurt in my chest and I want to cry all over. I'm not his girl. I won't ever be his girl. The ugly girl with the yellow hair downstairs is. I just know it. It's so unfair.

"I don't want dinner," I tell him.

"But your mom made your favorite chicken with the tomatoes and the cheese on top."

"Go eat it then," I gripe.

"Or . . . you could stop being a brat and tell me what's wrong," he snaps making me mad right back.

"You! You're what's wrong. Happy now?" I shout.

"What did I do, squirt? I'm always nice to you." He sounds so surprised. Like, can't he tell that he's breaking my heart?

"That's the problem!" I roll my eyes. Why is he so dumb? Are all boys this dumb?

"Why is my being nice to you a problem?" He laughs.

"Because you're nice to me and you have great

hair and I love you and you brought a girl!" I shout my eyes widen and I slap a hand over my mouth when I realize all that I just said before diving back under my covers. But Wes won't let me.

"Oh squirt," he sighs.

"Don't call me that," I whisper. "Please just go."

"No."

"Please," I beg.

"Sweet girl, you're ten years old and I'm eighteen. I can't love you back the way you want me to because that's wrong. I'm too old for you. I'm always going to be too old for you. But I can love you like a friend or a little sister. But that's it." I don't want to be Wes's little sister or his friend. This is terrible.

"Do you love her?" I ask knowing that I shouldn't.

"No."

"Good. She's not good enough for you." But all I could hear in my head was that Wes would never love me. That is was always going to be wrong for him to love me.

Beep . . . beep . . . beep . . .

"I can't lose her," I hear my dad cry.

"You're not going to lose her. She's sedated. That's all," I hear Wes reassure him. I want to open my eyes and tell them that I'm fine. I want to open my mouth but I can't. Wes said that I'm sedated but I don't know why.

"I can't lose another daughter this week," Dad sobs.

"You didn't know," Wes says, his voice grave.

"I didn't know. *I didn't know!*"

What is dad talking about? Another daughter? All I know is that I'm so, so tired. I need to sleep like I need to breathe. It's like I fell into the Hudson River and I'm being sucked down into the inky, black water. It's like when a murderer I was hunting this year shoved me over the bridge and down to the falls. I can't make my muscles move, I can't shout for help. I just sink down into the river until the blackness takes over.

This is it.

I won't take no for an answer. Wes and Liam are home on leave and I am not a little girl anymore. I am a newly minted, full-fledged woman of eighteen and have been for three whole weeks. Wes's argument that I am a little girl is invalid.

He's staying at his parents' place but they're in France this Christmas. It's the perfect opportunity to make Wes mine—guerilla warfare style.

I walk up the step and ring the bell. Wes answers the door wearing only jeans. His chest and feet are bare.

"Claire?" he asks when he opens the door but I jump through the opening and wrap my arms around his neck. I'm tall but he's taller so I have to pull him down to press my mouth to his in the kiss that I have been waiting my whole life for. And I have to do it quickly for two reasons: one, he will reject me if I give him a chance, and two, I might chicken out.

"Don't say no." I press my fingers to his lips to

keep him from talking before moving them out of the way to kiss him again. "Just don't say no."

Wes pauses for a minute, just standing there looking at me with my arms around his neck and my fingers twined in his hair. And then he moves. Wes pulls me into his arms and crushes his mouth down on mine before yanking me into the house and slamming the door shut behind me.

"I won't stop," he says when he pulls back to let me get a breath in. "Unless you need me to."

"I need you to not stop," I tell him.

"Then I won't."

I'm thirsty.

My mouth is so dry that it feels like it is full of cotton balls. It feels like I haven't had any water to drink in ages—lifetimes even. My eyelids feel like sandbags are holding them down. I'm sinking in quicksand and there is no way out but I have to fight it.

And I do.

I wiggle my fingers and arch my feet until a large hand clamps down over mine. I slowly blink my eyes once, twice, and the fingers grip mine again. Then I shake free the last of the weighted fog that held me down for however long and open my eyes.

"Dad," my brother says from next to me. "I think she's coming around."

"Claire," my dad says, his voice rough and pained.

"Dad? Lee? What happened?" I ask.

"You panicked," Liam says before clearing his

throat. "But you're okay now. You're alright."

"I'm alright," I repeat my brother's words like a parrot.

"Yeah, honey," my dad says blinking back tears.

"Wes was here," I say tasting the words like I'm not sure they're quite right.

"I'm right here, honey," the man in question says before pushing off the wall to walk up to me.

Wes brushes the hair back from my face. The way he's looking at me is so soft and so tender. It makes me want to believe that the feelings he spoke of were genuine. I know Lee said everyone kissed the strippers, but still. This gives me . . . *hope*.

"You're off this case," Lee says from beside me, ruining all of my warm and fuzzy feelings. I feel my mad growing stronger and stronger.

Wes sighs.

"What?" Liam asks.

"You couldn't give it like, say ten minutes before you start in on this shit?" We snaps.

"What are you talking about?" Liam shouts at Wes. "You were right here with me the last few days. You were just as upset as the rest of us."

"Because I love her too," Wes says, his deep voice rumbling.

"You want her off the case. You want her off the force just as much as I do." I hold my breath because he does—as much as Lee does—if not more.

Wes sighs again. He seems to do that a lot around me. "I want her to be safe, but I also want her to be happy. She's happy being a cop, I can keep her safe."

"You don't know that you can keep that promise,"

Lee grounds out.

"I will or I'll die trying," Wes promises.

"You better, brother," Liam says coldly and I startle at the tone in his voice towards his lifelong friend. "Or there will be consequences. Big ones. Lifelong friendship ending consequences."

We sit in tense silence for who knows how long. I feel nervous—edgy. So much so that I don't even want to move or speak let alone breathe or blink. There's a knock at the door just before it opens.

"Well, look who decided to join us today," an older doctor says as he walks in with a pretty nurse who winks at Liam and smiles sweetly at Wes.

"I guess that's me." I shrug.

They check me over up and down, top to bottom before declaring me fit for public . . . or well, resting outside of this hospital.

"We'll get some paperwork going and then you're free to go, Detective."

"Thank you." I practically bounce in my seat because hospitals have always given me the willies. I'm ready to get out of here.

"But you need to rest. No running around chasing bad guys just yet. Give it at least a few days."

"Sure," I say but we all know my fingers are crossed in my head.

It's not much but I'll take it . . . that is until I realize I have to go back to my apartment.

"Babe?" Wes asks.

"D-d-did they get it?" I ask hoping that he understands what I'm asking.

"Did they get what?" Liam asks and the room goes

wired.

"The snake," I whisper.

"He's gone, honey," Wes reassures me.

"Okay," I say, my voice small and pathetic.

"You're not going home either." Wes shares with us all and the room goes ultra-wired.

"Come again?" I ask tipping my head slightly to the side.

"You're coming home with me."

chapter 18

home again, home again, jiggity jig

"**W**HAT?" I ASK, I KNOW I couldn't have heard Wes correctly.

"You're. Coming home. With me," he declares and my brother looks a little maniacal with glee.

"No."

"And your attack is now under the investigation of the FBI," he states crossing his arms over his chest and challenging me with a stare down not to argue with him. So that's exactly what I do.

"I'll repeat, no." Hell has frozen over if Wes thinks I'm just going to let him take over.

"It's as good as done, Claire."

"You can't," I stumble over my words. I must have been out harder than I thought. "You can't just take-over this case."

"I can and I did."

"The original case is being handled by the GWT-PD," I challenge.

"It was. It's not anymore." Wes sighs before looking over his shoulder and then back at me before he speaks again. "Do you need help getting dressed?"

"No," I say petulantly crossing my arms over my chest. Wes lets out a frustrated breath.

"Everyone out." I look around—Lee, my mom and dad, my granny—they all stand around my hospital room or sitting in chairs, all with unhappy looks on their faces.

"Now, Son—" my dad starts but Wes cuts him off.

"No. Out *now*. Claire and I need to get a few things straight."

"I don't know that she's up to it," Liam adds softly. His eyes never leaving my face. I have to admit that it's nice to know that my brother has my back.

Wes rolls his eyes while I try and look my most pitiful. "She'll be fine."

Liam sighs before capitulating to his best buddy and leaving me alone. Benedict Arnold. "It'll be okay, Dad. And we'll be right outside if it's not."

"You're sure?" Dad asks Lee as he eyes Wes a little wary.

"Yes," Wes says emphatically.

"Yeah, Dad. I trust Wes and if he's wrong it's his funeral," he says casting me a sideways glance. At least I'm not losing my touch.

"Well . . . if you're sure," Dad hesitates.

"I am." And then they all shuffle to their feet and file out the door. Wes follows them shutting it firmly behind them and locking me in this room that's shrinking by the second—with one supremely pissed off FBI agent.

"Wes—"

"Oh no." He holds his hand up to me. "You do not get to lead me on a wild goose chase only to end up in the hospital and then tell me to take a hike. *Again*," he thunders. "I told you before, Claire. I am done fucking around. Done."

"Wes—"

"I've been living in hell since you wouldn't listen to me at the station. That was three days ago, Claire." Three days? I've been unconscious for three days? Holy shit.

"Umm . . ." I hedge.

"I didn't do anything wrong, Claire."

"I might have jumped to some wrong conclusions . . ." I admit.

"You think?" he thunders.

"Well—" I cringe.

"So, here's how it's going to be. You're going to come home with me." He ticks off on his fingers. "I am going to head up the investigation on an attack on a GWTPD Detective—that's you."

"Hey now!" I try to defend myself but clearly Wes is just getting started.

"No. I am doing this. I have to do this, Claire." I don't really know what to say to that, but by the sadness in his eyes and the pain that's written all over his face, I know that if I really love him—and I do—that I need to give him this.

"Okay," I say calmly.

"Okay?"

"Okay." I repeat.

"Third," he ticks off. "You and I will continue your investigation into the baby doll murders, together."

"The what?" I ask.

"While you've been in here the press did a big expose on the murders. They're calling them 'the baby doll murders.'"

"Shit."

"You got that right. They've been all over the GWTPD and the FBI. It's a nightmare. You're attack only added fuel to the fire." Shit. The last thing I want is to make the news again. When they talk about my cases and my police work, they love to make the jump to my disappearance. That was so long ago. Those vultures are incapable of letting sleeping dogs lie.

"Claire," Wes says as he steps forward. There is so much meaning and emotion packed behind his words that the air seizes in my lungs. He's just about to reach for me and I know that when he does, everything will change.

But then there's a knock at the door.

chapter 19

"**Y**OU READY TO GO, Detective?" the nurse asks as she walks into the room oblivious to the tension swirling in the air.

"Yeah."

"Fantastic. Now if you could just sign here acknowledging that we are releasing you from the hospital and if you have any of the following symptoms you will come back to the ER." The nurse instructs.

After I signed my life away, the nurse scoops up the papers and hands Wes a plastic bag with the hospital's logo on the side that contains all of my clothes and a shudder rolls up my spine. I hate the thought of that snake touching my clothes and I know in that moment that I never want to see them again. I wonder if it would be weird if I asked to wear the hospital gown home . . .

"Anna went and bought you some things to take to my house and to wear home until your apartment has been cleared by the crime scene unit. Which should be soon—but you don't have to go there anytime soon. Or I could just move your shit to my house and you never have to go there again." Wes says as if reading my thoughts.

"Umm . . ." I mumble.

"I see that might be too much too soon."

This time it was my turn to snap. "You think?"

"Anyway, here's an outfit. Let's get you dressed," he says effectively changing the subject by handing me two Target bags. I love Target!

Wes lifts the glossy white bags with red targets painted all over them from the chair in the corner. He pulls out a pair of panties and a jog bra, before pulling back the covers and slipping the blue gown down my shoulders.

Wes pulls the bra over my head and I slip my arms through. I don't see this caring side of Wes very often. I'm not sure if it's because I don't need it, or just that he doesn't like to show it. He hands me my underwear and I shimmy them up my legs while I sit on the bed. Then he pulls a pair of black yoga leggings out of the bag and rolls each leg up so that I can slip my feet in. He lifts me to the ground and crouches down so that he can pull my pants up. The gesture is so intimate and I don't know what to do about it.

Wes pulls a tank top and a zip up sweatshirt from the bag and slips the top over my head before holding the sweatshirt out for me to slip my arms into it. It's oversized on me and says NAVY across the chest. It was Wes's from back in the day and he knows how much I love it. When I was a kid I would make up any excuse to need to borrow it. I had always planned on stealing it one day. I love that he thought to bring it here to comfort me. He gently slides the zipper up the front of my sweatshirt to close out the cool spring air when we leave here.

Wes motions for me to sit back on the bed as he slides my favorite Converse sneakers onto my feet. The last two items were from Wes's house and I realize how intertwined our lives have become as he takes care of me in such a deep way.

Wes holds out a hand for me and helps me stand up. "Ready?" he asks.

"Sure."

"Claire—" he starts but I don't let him finish.

"I want out of here, Wes. I'm just not sure how I feel about my apartment or going home with you. It's been a rough year. You have to understand that." I explain.

"I do, baby. But you have to let me make it up to you. I need to take care of you." There's something in the way that he looks at me. I know—I would follow him anywhere. Wes will probably keep breaking my heart until the end of time, but I love him so much that I can't help but keep coming back for more. Whether I should or not.

"Then let's get to it."

Wes gently pulls me to my feet as if I'm the most precious and irreplaceable thing in the world, as if I'm made of spun glass. Even at my height he makes me feel soft and delicate. I love that. He brushes the hair back from my face before turning me around to face away from him. I want to ask him what he's doing but then his fingers sift through my hair separating it into three chunks before braiding it down my back. And then I'm hit with a memory.

When I was little I broke my arm when I fell off of my bicycle. I remember how frustrated I was that I couldn't get my wild hair out of my face. I was so upset that I couldn't get it up and out of the way so that I could continue to do whatever it was that I wanted to do to terrorize the neighborhood. Hot tears burned down my face with my frustration and my cheeks burned with embarrassment when Wes and Liam had found me sulking on the side of the house.

Wes had pulled me into his arms and hugged me. He had called me Squirt again like he always did and told me that I was too stubborn for my own good—and well, I always have been—before turning me around to face Lee who had pulled me into his arms with a soft smile on his face for his favorite sister while Wes began braiding my hair. Wes has always handled me with so much care and tenderness.

"Claire?" he asks breaking me free from my trip down memory lane. "Are you okay?" It's the first time in a long time that my memories haven't taken me down a dark and desolate path.

I let a smile break free on my face as I turn around and face him to say, "Yeah, I think I am."

"Okay," he says as he looks me over and I think for the first time in a long time that I really am alright and by the look on Wes's face he thinks so too.

"Let's go home."

Wes looks at me before looking at the plastic bag of the clothes I wore when the snake bit me and I see him notice me shudder. He tosses the clothes in a trashcan before turning to me.

"Now we can go." I knew I loved him for a reason.

"Thank you. But—" I start.

"Don't worry, I have your guns locked up in my safe at home." I nod to him before he motions to the door.

My family is all waiting in the hall but they don't say anything as we start to leave. I narrow my eyes on the nurse who brings a wheelchair around for me. Her eyes widen when she sees the expression on my face and then turns right back around.

Wes and Liam chuckle.

"Yeah, she'll be alright," my dad says.

Wes wraps his arm around me and pulls me into his side before leading me to the elevator. We ride down to the parking lot and Wes pulls open the door to his car for me to climb in. He buckles my belt and I'm not sure how I feel about this overly attentive side of Wes. I equal parts love it and hope it doesn't last long. Wes is already too overprotective. I need him to let me be me and love me at the same time.

The drive back to Wes's modest house is silent but he holds my hand in his on his muscular thigh the entire time. He parks in the driveway and then leads me inside. He closes the door behind us and turns the lock with a resounding click. It's the first time since we left the hospital that I realized I'm alone with Wes in his house. I have no car, no clothes, no gun. I'm at his mercy. And I'm not sure if I can forgive or forget yet. Or at all.

"Dinner or a bath?" he asks.

"A bath."

Wes takes my hand in his again and leads me slowly up the stairs and down the hall to where I know his bedroom waits. He doesn't flick on the light, but instead passes through the darkening room in its afternoon glow to the bathroom. Here he drops my hand in order to turn the taps in the bathtub to let the water begin to fill it up.

My mouth dries to dust when he slowly raises his hands to the plaque of buttons down the front of his shirt and one by one slides each button through the hole. I'm attracted to him, but then again, I always am. This isn't where our problems lie. But I'm also not sure that the answers can be found here either.

"What are you doing?" I ask when he peels the white fed shirt from his body and tosses it in the hamper by the door.

"Helping you with your bath." He doesn't make a move to take off the rest of his clothes. I breathe a little easier but I'm still not fully relaxed.

"I've been bathing myself since I was six years old," I inform him.

"This isn't that kind of bath," he says as he prowls towards me.

When Wes reaches me, he slowly slides the zipper of my sweatshirt down before sliding it down my arms and to the floor. He skims his hands down my sides to the hem of my tank top before gathering it in his hands and pulling it up and over my head.

"Wes," I whisper as he slides his fingers into my leggings and panties to shove them to the floor. Once I step out of them he sweeps me up into his arms like a bride and carries me across the bathroom when he gently sets me in the tub.

I settle back into the hot water and begin to relax as it seeps into my muscles. I crack one eye opened and watch Wes as he toes off his dress shoes and socks before padding back over to the tub where he kneels down beside me. He dips his hands into the water before grabbing a washcloth from the basket next to the tub and soaking it. Wes raises the washcloth up over my breasts and neck and squeezes out the water watching as it trickles down my body.

He does it again and again and I feel my body tingle as I watch the heat in his whiskey eyes blaze bright. I rub my thighs together like a cricket to ease some of the burn his gaze ignites. The water bobs around my breasts.

Wes drops the washcloth into the tub before trailing his wet fingers up my side while he leans against the tub. He cups the weight of my breast in his hand and I arch my back into him.

"Wes," I whisper. "What is this?"

"This is you takin' it easy."

"Hmm." Just when I think I can't take anymore and he'll give me what I want, what I need, Wes scoops the washcloths up from the bottom of the tub and squeezes some soap into it from the bottle on the edge of the bathtub. He gently washes my body like you would a child—definitely not taking the liberties with me that I have come to expect from him.

"Lean back," he says as I scoot down into the tub to dip my hair back to wet it. Wes scoops up water in his cupped palm and pours it over my hair before lathering shampoo between his hands and massaging it into my scalp. I close my eyes as the tension begins to leave my body.

"Hmm, that feels nice." I sigh as he leans me back into the tub to rinse the lather from my hair. When the water runs clear again Wes pulls the plug from the tub to let the water drain before lifting me out. He wraps me up in a big fluffy towel and I realize that, at least in this moment, maybe more, Wes is everything that I need.

"Hungry?" He asks me.

"No, you?"

"No, baby," he says as he brushes the wet mass of curls back from my face. I must look like a mess.

I grab my favorite t-shirt of Wes's out of his closet and put it on before hanging up the towel. I pull open his bathroom drawer and grab his comb to try and tackle the bird's nest that is currently my hair. Our eyes meet in the bathroom mirror and he smiles at me for no reason at all from where he casually leans against the wall watching me.

"What?" I ask.

"I like seeing you at home here, Claire," he says as he pads across the room to me. Wes takes the comb out of my hand and begins to work on my hair.

"Wes—" I start.

"I know you're scared, baby, but if you thought about it for more than a second, you would realize that you belong here with me." He takes a deep breath before pressing, on all while gently combing the knots from my hair as if I was more precious than a porcelain doll. "I'm not perfect and I've made a ton of mistakes with you. But I love you, Claire. You're it for me." My heart stutters and skips a beat over his words.

"What?" I ask. Wes drops the comb in the sink before turning me to face him.

"I love you. I have never loved anyone but you, Claire."

"I love you too, Wes." He closes his eyes and seems to savor my words before opening them again. He presses his mouth to mine in a hard but quick kiss.

"Good. Let's go to bed." I start to get excited. These kinds of proclamations come with sex, right? And right now, sex with Wes seems like a great idea especially after the lusty way he touched me in the tub before he just . . . stopped.

"Excellent idea," I purr.

"Good." He shuts off the lights and turns down the blankets before dropping his slacks and climbing in in his black boxer briefs that do something to me. "Goodnight, Goodnite." And then he grabs me and wraps me in his arms before closing his eyes. Umm . . . what?

"Wes?"

"Yeah, honey?"

"What are you doing?" I question him.

"Going to sleep.""Why?" I ask.

"Because you need your rest."

"Not that much." I narrow my eyes.

"Claire—" he starts but my name on his lips turns into a choking sound when I press my palm over his hardening cock.

I turn in his arms to face him pressing my mouth to his. This time I slide my hands down the front of his shorts and grip him tight in my fist before stroking him once.

"I'm fine, Wes." I stroke him again.

"You're sure?"

"Yes." I nod. "Now are you going to fuck me or what?"

"Yes, ma'am," he says before rolling me to my back and looming over me. He braces himself on his forearm by my head while he glides his other hand up my thigh and under his shirt where he finds me wet and wanting.

"Wes," I pant as he plunges a finger inside me. I stroke him harder and faster with my hand wanting him to lose just a little bit of the control he holds over himself but it's me who is quickly losing control.

"Is this what you need, baby?" He asks as he circles my clit with his thumb.

"Yes!" I cry out as I rock my hips into his hand but this isn't what I wanted. I want Wes and I want all of him. "No! I want you."

"Then you'll have me," he says as he slides his finger from my center and pushes the shirt higher on my chest where it's gathered just above my breasts.

I push his shorts down with my hands and he reaches between us to help me get rid of them before he tosses the fabric to the floor. Wes leans back down over me and I cradle his hips between mine. The tip of his cock parts me, dipping inside and we both groan.

Wes covers my body completely with his, framing my face with his hands. He looks in my eyes with so much love, so much emotion that my heart hurts to look at him in the very best of ways. I gasp when he slides deep inside me. Then, only then, does Wes make love to me. He does not fuck me like I asked, instead he slowly slides his body against mine as we ride wave after wave, whispering sweet love words to each other long into the night before drifting off to sleep held tight in each other's arms, twisted up tight in each other's hearts.

chapter 20

back at it

*I*T'S DARK. SO DARK. At night my mommy leaves a nightlight on for me and my favorite piggy stuffed animal that I've had for ages to help me sleep. I hate the dark. Monsters only lurk in the dark. I want my mommy but I can't cry. If I cry, the bad man will come and he will hurt me again. He always hurts me. Even though I don't want him to, I know, he always comes, but this time I will be ready.

I was digging in the closet when I knew that he was asleep. I found a pile of old junk. He must have been too lazy to clean out the closet that has been my prison for I don't know how long. But his laziness is my win. In the corner under the pile of old stuff, I found a baseball and then a glove, and in the very bottom of the pile, I found an old metal bat. Just like the kind Liam and Wes used when they were my age.

Sometimes it pays to be the little sister. My whole life I've been following Wes and Liam around hoping that they would play with me. I even told Wes that one *day he would marry me. He just laughed and said, "I'm not so sure about that, Squirt." That's what he calls me. Squirt.*

So, all the times, I followed them around when they played ball or walked in the woods is finally going to pay off even if Wes never wants to marry me. Because I learned how to swing a baseball bat watching them. I learned to run through the woods following them. I am going to run away from the bad man because of all that I watched them do.

So, I wait. And I wait and I wait and I wait. I almost fall asleep. Almost. I feel my eye lids getting heavy but then I hear footsteps and I know that he's coming. He always comes.

I sit quietly and try not to make any noise. Then hurry to my feet and grab my bat. I crouch in the corner with the bat over my shoulder just like Liam showed me how to do. When I hear the lock that he keeps on the closet door open I know that it's time.

My hands sweat and I feel shaky all over.

"Wake up, Claire, it's time," he says as he pulls open the closet door. "What are you doing?" He asks when he sees me but I don't answer. I swing the bat as hard as I can, hitting him in his big belly.

When the bad man falls forward, I swing one more time, hitting the side of his head just like Liam and Wes taught me to hit a baseball when I finally got them to include me. And then I run.

I run out of the closet while the bad man screams my name. I run out of the ugly house that smells funny and then I run out into the woods.

I run and I run and I run. But I know he's going

to catch me. A mean hand grabs me by my arm from behind and I scream . . .

The alarm on Wes's phone blares from the night stand beside me but I'm already awake. The dreams are changing and I'm not sure what that means. Maybe my fear is mixing with reality.

"Sleep, baby," he whispers in my ear before kissing me lightly just below.

"Umm . . . no," I say when he starts to rise from the bed.

"Honey, I have to go to work."

"I know," I say honestly, because I do. I totally understand and I don't want him to feel guilty, but I also need him to know that so do I. "I do too, Wes."

"No. It's too soon, Claire." He narrows his eyes on me.

"It's not and you know it. I'm fine, but I have to find out what's going on."

"The snake incident is under FBI investigation." I flinch as he intended for me to do at the mention of my gift. "That's what I thought, you're not ready."

"I am ready," I explain. "But I am never going to like snakes again."

"Not even this one?" he asks trying to distract me by pressing his hard length into my hip. I've decided to let him do just that for another thirty minutes or so.

"It's alright." I shrug.

"Alright? Just alright?"

"Yeah."

"I'll show you 'alright,'" he says as he smacks my ass flipping me to my hands and knees on the bed. I can't help the giggle that escapes my lips when I look back at him. "You naughty witch. Is this what you wanted?" he asks as he rises up on his knees behind me with his hard cock in his hand.

"Yes," I pant.

He runs his tip up and down against me and I arch into him trying to take what I want from him. He swats my ass again.

"Unh-uh."

"Wes."

"Say please."

"Please." Then he slams inside me so hard that the bed thumps against the wall. He plunges in hard again and again.

"You're so tight and wet, baby. And I love knowing that it's mine. It's all for me," he growls as he pounds into me.

"Yes," I pant. "It's all for you."

"Say it again."

"It's all for you."

I lay my cheek on top of my hands as they grip the sheets tight in my fingers. He sinks his cock into my center over and over with an urgency that took both of us over. My lips part on a gasp when he pinches my clit between his fingers. I moan out loud when he lets go and the blood rushes back all while he continues to pump hard and fast into my body.

"I want it, Claire. It's mine. Give it to me," he demands as he rubs my clit with his fingers. The sensations are overwhelming. I'm close but not there.

"Oh God, don't stop," I plead.

"Never."

"Don't stop."

"Never," he growls again. "I'll always give you what you need."

"I need it."

"I know." He pumps harder and harder as the bed bangs against the wall.

"I need to come."

"I know and I'm going to get you there." He pinches my clit again and I arch my back to take his cock and scream.

Wes pinches me again and I come. He roars my name before biting my shoulder where it meets my necks as he plants his cock deep inside me as he climaxes.

We're laying flat on the bed, me on my belly and Wes on top of me. My head is turned to the side so that I can breathe and my eyes are closed as I revel in the feel of Wes's hard heavy body on top of mine. He kisses the spot that he bit softly.

"Shouldn't have taken you so rough." I hear the sadness in his voice because he lost control and I won't have it. It was exactly what I wanted and more.

"Maybe it was exactly what I wanted," I tell him. "What I needed." He studies me before coming to some conclusion, I only hope it's the right one.

"You mean that."

"I do," I reassure him.

"I love you."

"I love you too." I smile at him. "Now, I need a shower before we can head out and so do you." He gives me a hard stare down.

"You'll stay with me?"

"Yes."

"You promise," he asks. He's not even trying to hide the fact that he doesn't believe me. That's annoying as hell but I don't want to miss my chance to get back out there. I need to get back on the horse and Wes and Liam need to see me do it too. If I don't do it now, it'll never happen so I weigh my words carefully.

"Of course." I reply as Wes narrows his eyes on me.

"Really?"

"Oh, for fuck's sake, yes! Yes, I swear I'll stick to your side like freaking herpes. Are you happy now?"

"Yes." The big bastard laughs. "To the showers!" he shouts as he swats my ass and takes off for the bathroom.

The surprise of the day goes to the tires on my department SUV for being slashed. I'll give it to Wes though. We walked out the front door of his house and there she sat in the driveway all flat and deflated.

"Well, there's that," he said before pulling out his cell phone and calling a tow truck to come and change all four tires.

"Mother fucker!" I shouted.

"Time to go to work," he declared as he herded me into is Fed-mobile and drove me to the station.

The ride to the station is eerily silent as Wes and I both mull over the facts in our minds. I can only think that I was getting close and that's why the killer left me the gift. I refuse to think of it as the creepy reptilian that it was. Or the fact that it was in my apartment.

Truth be told, I'm not sure which was a bigger violation.

Wes pulls into the parking lot of the station and cuts the engine. I can feel his eyes on the side of my face as I stare straight ahead—through the windshield to the glass doors and windows that cover the front of the building. I can tell that he's having regrets about bringing me along but I can't allow that so I unbuckle my seat belt. He lays his hand over mine to stay my movements.

"You're sure that you're ready?"

I nod once. "Yes."

He lets out a heavy sigh. "Okay." And then he moves his hand to unbuckle his own seat belt before climbing out of his unmarked sedan. I follow his lead and climb out too.

He pushes the door open and I duck under his arm to walk inside. Almost all conversation comes to a halt when everyone notices us. Officers I have known for years tip their chins in my direction as I head down the hall to the conference room that I had commandeered for my murder board almost a week ago before I was attacked.

I hate the word *attacked*. It makes me sound weak and helpless. I'm not a victim. I'm not. I protect the weak and the innocent. I fight for them and against the injustices they have been served. I am not weak. I am not a victim. But I was attacked. So now we have to find a way to link it all together to solve the case.

Wes pulls the glass door of the conference room open for me. It's a sweet gesture but in the moment, I'm not paying much attention to it. I'm focused on my murder board that's covered with photos, notes, and anything else that might be remotely relevant to the case.

I don't stop moving until my feet carry me to directly in front of the board. I place my palm to it and quietly pray for some kind of sign, some divine intervention, anything. I feel the weight of Wes's hand hit my shoulder pulling me back into the present.

"We're going to figure this out," Wes assures me.

"I have to, Wes. You don't understand."

"I do, honey. We're going to stop him." I nod my head in acceptance. I have to believe him. I can't constantly be looking over my shoulder and wondering where the bastard is, if he's still watching. This has to end. Soon. "Now, let's go over it again. From the top."

"Okay," I say moving to the start of information as it came it from the left side of the board. "Our first victim is Bonnie Bradley, age forty-one. Blonde hair, violet eyes. Divorced."

"The ex?"

"Not in the picture," I answer. "That's why she was dancing according to the other girls."

"The bouncer is a piece of work."

"Nah, he just wants to be one of us." I wink.

"No, he wants his dick to be one with your pussy and that's mine," he growls.

"Wes!" I scold.

"What? No one can hear us and you know that I'm right. He's into you."

"How should I know? I wasn't looking. May we continue?"

"Fine," he grumbles. He's so cute when he pouts.

"Thank you." I roll my eyes before continuing. "Second victim is Tammy Campbell. Twenty years old. Black hair, blue eyes. Works at the local coffee shop."

"Both victims dressed and posed in the same manner."

"Autopsy shows Bonnie was injected with Benzene to subdue her."

"That's not creepy at all," Wes says.

"Nope."

"Autopsy number two?" He sighs.

"Results should be in tomorrow. Emma is pretty reliable on time frame."

"Until then . . . what else do we have?" he asks.

"Let me show you."

Wes and I work long into the evening never stopping to eat or even leave the conference room. Wes and I go over every piece of evidence, every person of interest, with a fine-tooth comb. When the grit is so thick in our eyes that we can't stand it anymore Wes leads me out to the car waving to the night desk sergeant on our way out.

I can barely keep my eyes open in the car on the way home. In fact, I'm pretty sure I nod off from time to time. Thankfully, Wes doesn't live that far from my station so I haven't slept long when he pulls into the driveway and cuts the engine.

With slower than usual movements, we unbuckle our seat belts and climb out of the car. Barely noticing my newly fixed SUV sitting tall and proud on the other side of the driveway. Wes really did take care of me. Our limbs weighed down with a combination of exhaustion and frustration, side by side, Wes and I make our way up the walkway to the front door. I may already be half asleep again but as Wes stays my movement with a hand to my belly I am instantly awake.

"Stay here," he commands but all I can see is the gold and black movement on the front porch. The purr of its rattle has me immediately on alert.

Without thinking I pull my side arm from the holster at my hip and unload the clip—all sixteen rounds—into the swirling body of one big mother of a rattlesnake on Wes's front porch. It's body dances like the gunfighters in the old western movies finally coming to rest as the last bullet is spent from my chamber.

My gun is still raised as if that monster could come back from hell and wake up to torture me some more. I have to force the air into my lungs as I take a deep breath and the push it back out again. Wes slowly walks up to me and wraps his hand over the top of the gun, slowly pushing it down. It forces me to make all the muscles in my upper body relax.

"Well, I think it's safe to say that it's dead now," Wes deadpans from behind me I want to laugh but it's not funny. Tonight, I lost my cool and if Liam finds out he could take my badge for it once and for all. "Why don't you go back to the car and I'll call it in to dis-

patch."
    "Okay," I say embarrassment burning my cheeks.

chapter 21

freaking out

WES DOESN'T HAVE TO ask me twice.

After releasing my gun into his waiting hands, I turn to go back down the driveway but decide at the last minute to go wait in the house. I don't want to be standing out here like a lost little puppy when the cavalry arrives to see how far I have fallen. I follow my path around to the side of the house. I punch the code into the keypad on the door and let myself in. Wes gave it to me months ago. Yet, I have had few reasons to use it. We're always together.

At the time, I had told him he gives out a passcode so he can change it when he's done with the girl he was seeing. I teased him and said it was less messy than hunting down keys from women unwilling to part with them. Wes didn't correct me then and it's funny to me now that that is what is running through my head while I'm obviously being used as a play toy for a mad man. It also isn't lost on me that I don't currently have a key to Wes's house in my possession. I haven't been offered one either.

Love is a fickle bitch.

I walk through the house by memory, not stopping to turn on any lights. Instead, I make my way straight to the back windows in the kitchen that overlook the woods—woods that have haunted me almost my entire life—even now.

I know that Wes has to call in the incident. Not only did I fire my gun but the snake was obviously left by someone *for me*. Any minute this place will be crawling with Police Officers and FBI agents, but I need a quiet moment to collect my thoughts. Thoughts that are currently so jumbled that they are swirling around my brain so fast I can't seem to grasp onto any one of them at all.

Why?

The overall question I keep asking myself is why. Why is any of this happening? Why me? Or is it Wes? As far as I can see Wes is the only thing both Bonnie and Tammy have in common although only time will tell.

I don't know how long I stand there staring past my reflection in the dark glass. I must have missed the red and blue lights as they swirled up the hill—their sirens silenced as they made their way to Wes's beautiful home to ask the big questions. All of which include why.

I startle when Wes wraps his arms around me from behind. I close my eyes and hold my breath when he tightens his arms around me and gently places his mouth in the curve of my shoulder. I exhale when he tips his head up and rests his chin on my shoulder. I open my eyes to meet Wes's in the glass. I know what he's going to say even before the words leave his mouth.

"They're here, honey," he says softly.

"I know."

"Lee's here too," he informs me in a gentle voice.

"Okay," I say out towards the dark night behind the glass.

"So is your dad." I don't say anything just nod. I should have known that this would happen. I can't keep the secrets no matter how hard I try and the truth is I'm freaking out. "He's worried. So am I." "I know." I feel the tears burning behind my eyes and I would do anything right now to keep them from falling.

"Do you want to talk about it?" he asks me, his tone laced with the worry I see mirrored in his eyes.

"No, I just want to answer their questions. That's going to take long enough. Then I want to go home and go to bed." He stiffens at my mention of going home.

"You are home, Claire. For the night at least..." The timbre of his voice leaves no mystery to his purpose. Wes is gearing up for a fight. He's digging in his heels.

"Wes—"

"Like you said, this is going to take all night so let's go answer their questions."

"Sure," I say for lack of anything better. "Let's go."

Wes unwraps himself from around me and holds his hand out. I know I shouldn't, but I can't help myself, I pause looking at his hand. He deserves so much better than the broken half person I am. And before I have a chance to take it, Wes sighs with deep frustration before turning to walk out the door.

At this juncture, I have no choice but to follow.

We walk back through the house—which is now lit up like the Christmas tree in Rockefeller Center—back to the dining room. I'm not sure how often Wes has ever entertained in this room, but here it is with his huge oak table that seats over twenty people and his matching upholstered, high back chairs. My dad sits in one of the chairs. He's staring at his hands that rest on top of the table. Liam is pacing around the room like a caged tiger. I already know what his response will be.

I'm about to get canned.

"Sit down, Claire," Liam says to me when he notices me enter the room.

"I'm good where I am, Lee. Just spit it out," I say as I fold my arms across my chest. He stares at me from across the dining room. Lee's stance is mirroring mine as he studies me as I study him.

"Oh, for fuck's sake I'm not firing you! Just sit the fuck down!" he yells.

"You're not?" I ask. I'm as shocked as I sound right now.

"No!" he snaps. "Am I worried about you? Yes. Am I going to let some sicko grab you? Fuck no. So, sit down and let's get to the bottom of this."

"Okay," I say as I start to sit down.

"Wait!" He yells and I freeze with my ass only partially lowered to the chair as Lee makes his way through the room to me. He pulls me up out of the chair and hugs me to his chest. "I love you, Claire Bear." Tears spring up in my eyes at his use of my childhood nickname. I hug Lee back tight before shoving him away and roll my eyes.

"You're so stupid," I say shooting him a weak smile before sitting down. Wes stands guard behind me. His presence reminds me that I'm not alone—at least not right now. Right now I have him in my corner and it feels really good. Even if I don't deserve it, I'm going to take it.

I take a deep breath and look around the room. Cruz is talking with Jones. They look absolutely pissed that this is happening. We take care of our own in our department and they're both very protective of me. There are a bunch of suits looking nervous—one man and one woman, Agent Procter and Agent Webber—probably because someone planted a snake at their boss's house for him and his girlfriend to find. And lastly, Anna and Emma are speaking in hushed tones in the front of the house.

"Can you tell us what happened?"

"We left the station and drove ho-here." I catch myself just before I refer to Wes's house as home. I see the smirk on Lee's face as he catches my blunder—the bastard.

"We were going to make something quick or order a pizza," Wes chimes in. "This case has been brutal. We spent all day at the station catching up on it, going over the details again."

"And then what?" Liam questions.

"As we were walking up to the front door we noticed the snake."

"And then what happened?"

"I-I-I . . ." I can't get the words out. They're frozen in my mouth which is locked down tighter than Riker's Island. I can't tell this room full of people—my peers, people that I *love*—that I panicked. I choked. I freaked out.

"It's okay, Claire. You can say it," my dad tells me as he lays his hand on top of mine.

"It scared me and I lost it," I admit.

"What scared you, Claire?" Anna asks as she and Emma move closer into the dining room. I hate that she's asking me on record about what startled me. But she is and this is where we are now.

"The snake."

"And then what happened?" my dad asks.

"Wes called to me to stop but I wasn't paying attention. And then when I got to the porch, I saw it."

"And what did you do when you saw the snake?" Liam asks.

"I shot it."

"How many times did you shoot the snake, Claire?" Liam questions.

"I emptied my gun," I whisper ashamed that a stupid non-poisonous snake would startle me.

"It's gone now, honey," Wes says softly placing his warm hand on my shoulder and giving me a squeeze. He's infusing me with some of his warmth whether he knows it or not.

"I mean it's so silly that it would rattle me so much. Get it? Rattle me . . . because it was another de-venomed rattlesnake." Emma and Anna look to each other and then to Liam and Wes. And then back to each other. Emma shakes her head no.

I'm missing something here.

"Wait. The snake wasn't poisonous, was it?" I shudder thinking of the snake that bite me in my apartment and how this one could have done the same.

"Claire," Liam says softly.

"After she shot the snake, I told Claire to go into the house through the side door using my personal passcode to disable the lock and alarm while I phoned it in. That was where she was when I came in to tell her that the troops had arrived," Wes adds trying to change the subject but I can't let him do that. I can't let them baby me. It might be coming from good intentions or it might not. With Wes and Liam, I don't know, but this is my life and I will always fight for control of it.

"No," I demand. "Someone tell me what's going on here. Anna? Emma?"

"It was poisonous," Emma says point blank. Crime Scene said the glands were intact and the specimen had not been milked recently either."

"What?" I shake my head at her science geek speak. "Stop. Just say it so it makes sense."

"The snake was poisonous. Very poisonous," she adds at the last second. The room is silent as we all take in just how serious this is getting.

"I think that's all we need for now," Lee says closing a notebook before he stands from his seat at the large table. "I think I speak for everyone from both agencies when I say if you two want to take a day off tomorrow, everyone will understand."

"No!" I shout. "I'll be there. This monster has scared me from two homes. I won't let him take work from me too."

"Okay," Lee says as he pulls me into his arms again. "I love you, kid."

"I love you too, fart breath," I say into his chest.

"Take care of her," he says to Wes as he reaches out to shake his hand.

"Always."

Lee looks anywhere but at Emma and Anna standing just inside the dining room which is super awkward since he has to pass by them *closely* to leave. I'm assuming he's going to manage the pack up and move out of the crime scene techs, the detectives, and the feds.

"Asshole," Emma whispers loud enough for everyone to hear while Anna looks sick to her stomach. *Interesting*. And unfortunate.

My dad stands up to follow him out, only stopping to hug me and Wes.

"She's my little girl, Wesley. Protect her."

"With my life." Dad nods once and then follows Liam out the door. The detectives follow closely on his heels.

"I'll be okay," I say when I see Emma and Anna move closer to me. "Everything looks better after a good night's sleep."

"Claire—" Anna starts but I interrupt her.

"No, it's fine. I didn't survive everything that I did so that this asshole can take me down. I'll be vigilant, I swear." Anna opens her mouth to argue with me but Emma stops her with her hand to Anna's arm.

"That's all we can ask." Anna pauses before seeming to agree with Emma. They both hug me and then follow my welcome home party outside.

When the last person had left, Wes shuts the door behind them and lets the locks tumble into place. He turns around, leaning his back against the front door and watches me. Whatever he seems to see, I'm not sure that I want to know. Tonight, I was forced to let it all hang out and that's not very becoming. Let's face it, I'm a mess.

"You hungry?" he asks me.

"Not even a little bit."

"Good. Me either," he says. "Let's go to bed." Wes walks towards me and holds out his hand. I gladly take it.

"Okay, honey," I say softly, my eyes on his and he smiles at the outward show of trust that I'm handing him on a silver platter.

"A wise woman once said that everything will look better after a good night's sleep." He winks.

"Oh, I have a regular wise guy on my hands, huh? Cracking jokes . . ."

"Definitely." He smiles. "Besides, it's always a good night when I get to fall asleep with you in my arms."

"Okay, Romeo. Let's go to bed."

"Now, you're talking."

And we do just that. Wes and I do not make love. We do not kiss or touch as we ready ourselves for sleep. We do not talk about our day or our feelings as we pull the sheets and blankets back on the bed and climb in. It is obvious that there is a slew of emotions riding both of us hard right now and we do not share any of them. Instead we lay down in the huge bed, me on my side facing the window that looks out over the back of the house. Wes is behind me. He snuggles in close, his knees nestled behind mine. Wes drapes his arm around my waist and slides his other arm under the pillow beneath my head after pulling the blankets back up over us.

"I love you, Claire," he says before I feel his body slowly slip into sleep.

I do not respond.

I continue to stare out the window into the dark night. What monsters lurk out in the trees and moonlight? I wish I knew because then I could stop them. But also, I don't because I'm so afraid of what those monsters might look like in the daylight. Everything is scarier in the daylight.

Right now, I have nothing but questions with no answers. I force myself to relax each muscle in my body one by one and close my eyes before finally allowing myself to sink into the nothingness of sleep.

Here's hoping tomorrow will be brighter. Too bad that it won't. I just wouldn't realize it until later, much later. Some monsters only come out in the day time.

chapter 22

why you

EEP . . . BEEP . . . BEEP . . .

Wes reaches over to shut off the alarm clock on his side of the bed and I'm beginning to feel like I'm trapped in that movie, *Groundhog's Day*. I want to pull the pillow over my head and hide under the blankets, I want to wait until all of this is over to come out from hiding, but part of me knows that this isn't going to end without me being an active participant. For some reason, everything seems to be circling around Wes. I just can't wrap my mind around why.

This morning is different from the last.

There is no laughter, no light banter. And definitely no wild morning sex. But also, no nightmares. I guess I should be thankful for small favors. Instead we both peel back the covers feeling every bit of the exhaustion we have accrued over the last few days. Without speaking a word to each other, we dress for work, me in jeans and a sweater that I top off with boots and my backup weapon—seeing how my service weapon was surrendered last night pending the investigation of my shooting the rattlesnake on Wes's front porch. Wes dresses like every inch of the fed that he is in another one of his gray suits—striped tie and all.

We don't stop to make coffee or eat breakfast. We both know that there is no use arguing over it. I need to get to the station. I need to do more interviews. Go over the evidence again. Something is missing and I won't be able to rest until we figure out what it is. We both won't be able to rest until we figure out what it is. That's the nature of our occupations, but also, it's just the nature of us, of Wes and Claire. We have always needed to find the answers that weren't always visible. We always asked the questions others wouldn't dare to.

So, we climb back into Wes's fed car, the one that drove us home last night. And there's that word again. *Home*. That's not the first time I caught myself referring to Wes's house as home. It was awkward as hell when it almost slipped out while giving my statements to the police and the feds. Everyone heard me stop myself, I know it. I could see the acknowledgement on their faces, the recognition that I'm in too deep and realizing it. Especially with everything constantly coming back to Wes at every turn.

So now I'm questioning everything else. Including Wes.

I'm itching to run as he pulls the car into a parking spot in the lot at the station. I'm damn near desperate to put a little real estate between us. Basically, I need some space to sort out this case and my head. But I also know that is the last thing Wes will grant me. It's really starting to suck that I know him so well.

"I'll understand if you need to head to your office for a bit," I hedge. Wes narrows his eyes on me.

"In a hurry to get rid of me, are you?"

"No!" I answer just a little too quickly.

"You're not going to run from me again, Claire. I thought I made that perfectly clear the last time you tried it." This time I narrow my eyes on Wes.

"You don't own me, Wes," I growl. "I am my own person. For fuck's sake, I'm a respected and decorated police detective!"

"I know all that," he rumbles low in warning like a wolf I've just pissed off. "But I do own you, baby. I own every part of you from that long, dark hair I love to wrap my fist around, to your heart you keep so heavily guarded, down to your sweet as fuck pussy and all the fucking way down to your toes that you love to keep painted pink. I own every bit of you just as you own every bit of me and I always have. So get fucking used to it." With that he gets out of the car and slams the door closed—which only moves to piss me off. I'm sure Anna would tell me that I'm avoiding the highly romantic declaration Wes just made by being pissed the fuck off. So, I step out of the car and slam my door too.

"And I'm a fucking grown up!" I yell.

"Then fucking act like one!" he shouts back as he pulls open the glass door to the station for me.

"Well aren't you just a merry fucking ray of God damned sunshine this morning!" I holler as I step into the lobby of the station for all to hear.

"Yeah!" he shouts right back at me after the door slams closed behind us. "I'm having a great fucking day! I get to follow my girl around. Again! While she chases a killer all while hoping the woman I'm in fucking love with doesn't get fucking killed before I have a chance to ask her to fucking marry me! So yeah, it's gonna be a great fucking day!"

The bullpen is so quiet at Wes's outburst that you could hear a pin drop.

"What?" I ask. I had no idea he was serious about me. About us. That he was considering marriage. Holy fuck.

"Hey!" Liam shouts from his office. "Ralph and Alice, mind getting your fucking asses into my Goddamned office before you knock each other to the moon!"

"Fuck!" Wes bites out.

"Wes—" I start.

"Not. Now." I just nod, not sure what else to do. I'm so lost.

We make our way down the hallway and Liam is standing there holding the door to his office open for us. Like naughty children on their way into the Principal's office we drag our feet in single file, one after the other, with our heads hanging in shame. Well, Wes's probably is. I have no shame and we all know it.

Liam follows us in and slams the door shut.

"Nice *Honeymooners* impression kids," he says holding up his thumb and index finger about an inch apart. "I am this close to pulling you from this case, Claire. I could suspend you for this shit, *without pay*."

"Now, hold on, Liam—" Wes starts but doesn't let us finish.

"Don't even start with me, Wes." Lee shakes his

head. "Do you get that I can have your agency banned from this station for the shit you two are pulling? That your behavior is fucking embarrassing?"

"I'm sorry," I say sadly. "It's my fault. All of it. Don't blame Wes."

"You guys are so annoying with your ups and downs and at each other's throats and then defending each other. It's exhausting!" Liam whines. I roll my eyes. "Just get your shit together when you're here. That's all I ask."

"Okay," I say. "I'll lose my shit at home."

"I love it when you call my place home, baby."

"God damnit, I didn't!" I back pedal. "I was talking about my apartment."

"You should really consider moving in with me this weekend," Wes says and Liam nods. "It would make everything better."

"How would our not having our own space make anything better when we're already at each other's throats?" I ask.

"Because then you can fuck me whenever you want," Wes says on a wicked smile.

"Gross, dude, that's my sister," Liam says looking a little green around the gills.

"The idea does have some merits," I play up to annoy my dickhead of a brother.

"Gross. Are you done yet?" Liam rolls his eyes.

"And think about all the times I could eat you on the kitchen table," Wes adds helpfully.

"I've eaten at that table, fucker! I think I'm going to be sick," Lee complains. I can't help but laugh.

"Seriously, Claire. Think about it?" Wes pleads.

"Oh fine! I'll think about it. But only because you are so pathetic." I throw my hands up in exasperation.

"I am. Thank you." Wes smiles at me.

"Good now that that's all settled do either of you have anything to add?" Lee asks and then quickly speaks again before either Wes or I can say something else to gross him out. "I mean about the case!"

Just then the phone on his desk rings.

"Goodnite," Lee says as he answers the phone. "Yeah, they're both here . . . Okay, I'll let them know." He lowers his voice so that Wes and I can't hear what he's saying but after a lifetime of being his little sister, that only makes me listen harder. "Then we need to talk about this . . . but it did happen . . . I don't care . . . we will talk about this!"

Liam holds the phone out in front of his face as is he can't understand what just happened. The dial tone sounds through the small room and it's evident that whoever it was hung up on him. He closes his eyes and shakes his head to clear it before hanging up the phone. I look to Wes and his face is carefully blank. Whatever just happened, he knows more than me and that is totally unacceptable. The Bro Code is bullshit.

"That was Emma, she has your autopsy results ready and said she's free to go over them now if you guys want to head on down to the basement." I arch an eyebrow at him. So that was Emma he was talking to in angry hushed tones. Interesting.

"Yeah, I'll get right on that." I smirk at my brother on my way to the door. I need to do some serious investigating over this shit. Too bad I have to catch a killer first.

"I could still suspend you, Goodnite," he shouts from his desk.

"You could try! But I'd tell mom on you," I call out as I leave his office.

"God damnit," he grumbles. Wes just laughs as he follows me out the door.

This one is special.

This one is different from all the rest. This one has actually fucked him. I could tell by the way she watches him. The way she watches him with her.

There's a sadness in her eyes.

He doesn't deserve her or this one. But this one has to die.

She's almost perfect. But not. She has eyes the color of violets and hair like a raven's wing. But her face is wrong. Her nose turns down instead of up. There are no freckles across the bridge of it. Her body has more bulky muscle—not much—but enough that it's noticeable that she is not the one that I want.

But she fucked him when he wanted her. They lie to her every day about what happened and she has no idea. Yet, she still chooses him! How could she be so stupid? I have given her everything and still she goes to him every fucking time.

Last night I left her a snake as a punishment. How I hoped it would strike her the way I want to. It's fangs slipping into her skin the way I will slip in the needle. Soon. It'll be soon, Claire.

But not yet.

This one approaches as she walks back through the restaurant where she stopped for lunch. She still goes to the same restaurant every day that she dined with him in while they were together. Hoping he'll come back for her. But he doesn't. He never will.

She steps outside and I'm waiting over by where she's parked.

"Oh hey, it's you," she says when she recognizes me.

"Hey, it's you too." I smile at her. "Hey, I've been thinking about something . . . do you mind if I ask you a question?" I say as I step closer to her, just inside her personal space.

"Sure. Ask me anything," she says nervously. Her pupils dilate. Her instincts are telling her that something is off, that something is wrong. And they are correct.

"Why couldn't you keep him?" I ask as I jab the needle into the side of her neck and push down the plunger.

The effect of the benzene is almost immediate. Her body goes limp and her eyes go wide in panic. She can't even open her mouth to scream for help. I smile at her.

"You?" she whispers. I just smile indulgently at her.

"Don't worry, this will be over quickly."

I drag her towards the back of the lot. It's terribly unsafe here. No cameras, it's dark and dingy. You would think it would be safer with so many FBI agents around, but tragically it's not. I sigh. The world can be so cruel.

Tears slip free from the corners of her eyes as I

strip her of her ugly suit and gun. I lick them from her cheeks. I need to taste her fear, her helplessness, and the realization that loving a man that she couldn't have is what ultimately cost her life.

"If only you had kept him," I say sweetly. "We wouldn't be here."

I unbuckle my belt and unzip my slacks. My cock is hard and just free from my pants. It's because she's almost perfect. This one might be the last one before we claim her. The thought makes the tip seep with pleasure and I can't help but close my eyes and stroke myself with my fist before.

"You should be pleased," I say as I dress her in the brown floral dress I made for her myself. She's beautiful in it. She'll be just like a doll. "You're almost perfect."

I straddle her and rub my cock against her pussy. A groan slips free. She feels so good. I brace my hands on her shoulders and drive into her, impaling her on my dick. I can't stop myself as drive myself closer and closer to climax.

I wrap my hands around her neck and she closes her eyes. This one knows that the end is near. I drive in one more time as my cum fills her body and I squeeze the life from her.

I pull out and stand while zipping up my pants. I'm disappointed that she distracted me so much I forgot to use a condom but I don't let it frustrate me too much. By the time the police figure out who I am, I'll have already taken her and I will be long gone. Again. Just like last time and the time before that.

I turn this one onto her side and place her hands

up under her cheek in prayer position. I don't have to close her eyes for her and that's kind of a fun change. Although, I prefer to watch their eyes when they realize they are dying.

I stop to take one last look at her. She looks perfect. Almost. And then I turn and walk away.

My belly is full of butterflies as we ride in the steel box down to Emma's lair. Our arrival is sounded by a ding as the doors swing opened.

"Where the hell have you two been?" she shouts from her desk. "I called. Like a ton."

"We were in a meeting with Liam," I say casually.

"I know," she says, her frustration clear in her voice. "That's where I found you."

"So, you found us . . . What were you and Liam talking about on the phone?"

"I have no idea what you're talking about," she snaps before looking around nervously. Uh-huh, sure. I'll believe that. It was nothing. "Besides, I have your autopsy results."

"Okay, show me."

"Victim: female, age nineteen identified through fingerprints as Tammy Campbell. Brown eyes, black hair. The color is natural, no dyes."

Interesting. I'm not sure how I feel about that. She can't be my long-lost sister too, that would be ridiculous. Too coincidental.

"Her stomach contents contain a bagel and coffee which is consistent with her employment at a coffee shop. There was vaginal tearing and condom lubricant found during exam."

"Cause of death?" I ask.

"Good old strangulation. But wait! There's more." Emma says in her game show host voice.

"Such as?"

"Your victim was subdued with an injection of benzene. Needle marks found in the shoulder area."

"Just like Bonnie Bradley," Wes adds from his spot next to me.

"Exactly!" Emma claps.

"But who? Who is doing this shit?" I ask. I hate that I can't figure it out. I hate that there's a serial killer in my fucking town killing women that look kind of like me. That shit is creepy as hell.

My frustrating thoughts are interrupted but Wes's ringing phone.

"Agent O'Connell," he answers. "Say again? . . . You've got to be shitting me." Wes turns with his back to Emma and I. He has one hand holding his phone to his ear and the other is clenched in a fist at his hip. His feet are braced apart and his hold body radiates tension. His anger ripples across his broad back.

"Wes," I whisper but he's too busy yelling at the person on the other end of the phone.

"Nobody touches anything until I get there. Especially not the PD!" he shouts before hanging up his phone and stuffing it back into his pocket.

"Wes?" I ask again.

"I have to go. *Do not* leave this station," he barks out before jabbing the button for the elevator. The doors open immediately and he walks through the steel doors without ever looking back. I can't help but feel like everything just went to shit.

I'll find out later that it really just did.

chapter 23

just like you

*L*OOK BACK. *LOOK BACK. God damnit, look back!*

I'm damn near shaking as I plead with Wes to look back at me, to give me anything at all, but he doesn't he just walks away. No, Wes stormed away after issuing me an order not to leave the station. He didn't even kiss me goodbye.

I know I shouldn't care, that I shouldn't need his reassurances, but something happened and God dammit I do! I do need them. I have no idea how long I stood there staring at the elevator doors with tears burning the backs of my eyes before Emma voices my exact thoughts.

"What the fuck just happened?"

"I-I have no idea," I whisper.

"It'll be okay, honey", she says as she rounds her desk and puts her arms around me. Emma is as tall as I am and her arms are strong—so she hugs the breath right out of me. In our little unlikely trio, Anna is the shorty. She calls us, "Two talls and a small."

"I just don't know."

The phone on her desk rings and she squeezes me one more time before walking back around to answer it. Our department isn't exactly loaded so we have old fashioned black phones on our desks that look like they're straight out of *Get Smart*. Sometimes that's exactly how it feels. Like we're stuck in a slapstick comedy routine, I just haven't found the punchline yet.

"Parker," she answers before listening. "Where? . . . Awe isn't that sweet, you're calling me in. You know who I work for . . . If you think I'm neutral territory you're a bigger moron than I had originally thought." With that she slams her phone back down in the cradle and looks to me with wide, unsure eyes. Before I have a chance to ask her what happened my cell phone is ringing in my jeans pocket.

"Goodnite," I answer.

"Goody, this is Cruz. We've got another body."

"Where?" I ask.

"Down at the Greek Cafe over on third."

"I'm on my way. Make sure the crime scene is secure," I bark out as I head for the elevator and jab the button with my finger.

"About that," he hedges.

"Yeah?"

"We got a problem." The pause after he speaks is pregnant with all of the department bullshit.

"That's not something I want to hear, Cruz," I tell him after a moment.

"The Feds tagged this one."

"Nope, not possible. This is our case. This is *my*

case," I growl.

"*She's one of them*," he says softly so only I can hear it.

"Who?" I ask, the pit of dread in my stomach taking up more and more room.

"*Agent Webber*." The female agent that was at the house last night looking worried and very uncomfortable to be in Wes's house. Damn it!

"Shit," I bite out.

"*Yeah*."

"I'm on my way," I say and hang up as the elevator doors ding opened.

Then I realize that I don't have my fucking car here because I've been riding with Wes. *Wes*. That asshole who took off after declaring that whatever happened did not go to the PD—*my fucking department*—and then demanded that I not leave this station. He is un-freaking-believable.

The elevator doors have just closed when I push the button to open them again. When they swing opened Emma is standing there looking at me with a smirk on her pretty face.

"I need a cab," I shout.

"You going my way, pretty police lady?" she asks on an evil cackle. Emma is definitely one to bust your balls but in the nicest of ways.

"Yes," I say emphatically. "I'll even put out."

"Fantastic!" she cheers. "Get in the van."

Damn. I hate the van. It's the Medical Examiner's body mover van and it gives me the willies. I make the sign of the cross over my body before following her out of her morgue and into the back-parking garage where they keep it.

"Pussy!" she snickers.

"Fuck you." I laugh.

The drive over to the Greek Cafe would have me a nervous wreck under normal circumstances. I hate it when we lose one of our own regardless of department or agency. At the end of the day it all boils down to we're just different kinds of cops.

However, Emma likes to shake the newly dead with classic rock at the highest decibel she can tolerate. Today is AC/DC. She did a nice segue from *Hell's Bells* to *You Shook Me All Night Long*. Classy as fuck if you ask Emma. But what it does do is help me maintain a certain level of calm.

Well, as calm as one can be while in an ME's body mover van while said ME is driving like a nineteen-year-old lunatic who was just handed the keys to daddy's Porsche. Hand to God, I swear she took the last turn on two wheels and then pulled into the parking lot of the Greek Cafe with screeching tires.

As soon as the car stopped, I jumped out and almost hit the grass on my knees praying for the safety of all around her and screaming "Land!" But I decided that was probably a bit much. Instead, I pulled my badge from my hip and held it up to any Fed that might think they can boot me from this scene.

I see my officers huddled over by a tree, standing in various poses of pissed off, one with his arms folded across his chest, another with hands on his hips and feet spread. All with scowls on their faces. I'm making my way to them when I'm stopped by a hand on my arm.

"I wouldn't do that if I were you," I seethe.

"This isn't your crime scene, Goody," the male agent from last night says. Agent Procter, I believe.

"That's not what I heard."

"The boss won't want you here," he snarls at me and I find that very interesting. Up until now, we've been mostly together investigating this case.

"And why is that?" I ask.

"Because he and Tawnya had a thing." It's like a fist to my gut and I know he sees it, he delivered the blow with unfailing accuracy. I just can't understand why. Either way, it knocked the wind out of me.

"Excuse me?"

"You heard me," he says, his voice low. "He needs time to grieve. If you ever cared for him at all, give him that."

Obviously, he doesn't know me because I think not.

"Take your hand off me, Agent Procter."

"Don't say I didn't warn you," he sneers.

I make my way over to the officers and detectives that I know. I see that they caught my . . . *disagreement* with the Fed. Well, that can't be helped now and it looks like we'll have to move quickly to take control of this crime scene. I so love a good pissing contest with the stuffed suits.

"Alright, guys," I say taking a deep breath before pressing on. "Tell me what we got."

"We have the body of a female, mid-thirties, dressed in an old timey dress and posed to be sleeping. Victim has been positively identified as Federal Agent Tawnya Webber," Jones recites from his notes.

"At which time the feds gave us the boot," Cruz adds.

"Not for long boys," I say with confidence I am not currently sure is real or not, but right now I'm going to go with it. I put my fingers to my mouth and let out a shrill whistle. "Listen up! We at the George Washington Township Police Department would like to thank you finely dress suits for showing up and pissing all over my crime scene, but you are dismissed. Effective immediately! Emma, your team doesn't touch shit until my guys get a good look."

"You got it, girl!" she cheers like a looney tune.

"Now see here," Agent Procter who dropped the little Wes and Tawnya sitting in a tree with naked genitals bomb shouts. "This is Federal jurisdiction.

"Since when?" I shout back. "I have two bodies that match this one. This is mine. So, get your shit and get out."

"And clearly, you're doing a right fine job with them," he sneers. The fucker. My guys visibly bristle and start to move towards the jerk to pound his face in. I would love nothing more myself, but it won't win us the battle at hand so I put a hand out to stop Jones and smile my brightest smile.

"I'm sure glad you think so. You know we've just been working so hard on this case while you've been shining your wingtips so you can go right on ahead and get back to that now. Okay, thanks, bye!" I wave.

"Handle this, O'Connell!" he shouts.

"Ooooh, nice one!" I snap my fingers. Before motioning to my officers. "Move in guys. I want everything. I want to know what she ate last, her mother's maiden name, and who she fucks at night." I add that last one just to see if I can get a reaction out of anyone and I definitely do when Wes cringes. *Awesome.*

"Yes, ma'am." The all file out.

"Claire," Wes growls as he stalks towards me.

"Speak of the Devil. Say his name and he shall appear," I say under my breath.

"I thought I told you to stay put at the station," he growls.

"Yeah, about that, I didn't." I shrug.

"I can see that. But why?" he bites out.

"Because I have an active crime scene to go over," I answer honestly.

"This is my crime scene, Claire. Back off," he warns.

"No can do, Buckeroo." I shrug. "One, this matches two of my crime scenes and you know that. Two—" he cuts me off.

"She's one of my agents. This case is now mine," he thunders.

"She's also your lover, this case is not yours and if you push me, I will go to Lee and see that he backs my claim."

"You'd play your brother against me?" he seethes

"I'm sure he knows all about your history with Agent Webber. It's the right thing to do and you know it. For one reason or another, this case is all about you."

"It's not what you think, Claire," Wes pleads, changing tack.

"I don't care about what I think. I care about facts and finding the killer before he kills anyone else," I say with a calm I do not feel.

"Claire, you have to listen to me," Wes pleads.

"No," I stop him. "Don't say anything. I expect you in the station by five this evening for questioning."

"Don't do this, Claire."

"You can either surrender yourself for questioning or I can have an officer bring you in." I take a breath before leaning in to whisper. "Please do not make me do that."

He whispers back, "It was before you."

"Then let me do my job. I promise we'll take good care of her." He closes his eyes and nods at my words before turning and walking away.

I make my way to the body where Emma and her team are taking pictures and marking evidence.

"What do we have, Emma?"

"We have a female victim, mid-thirties, black hair and violet eyes." I had a feeling. For whatever reason, this killer is targeting Wes but the physical similarities are staggering.

"Natural?" I ask.

"Hair yes, eyes are contacts, but . . ." Emma answers but then lets her voice trail off.

"But what?" I ask suddenly feeling incredibly tired.

"I have to say . . ." I know what's coming. I steel myself for it even as I make my spine go straight, standing taller with my shoulders back, I hold my breath and look her in the eyes. But no matter how much I brace for it, I know that I'm not ready to take that blow too. "She looks just like you."

chapter 24

before you

IT'S A SLAP TO the face.

No, it's not. Hearing that this woman who I know Wes was intimate with—and even though I don't know the nature of their relationship, did he love her? Did she think of marriage? Was it just a cold, hard fuck? I don't know, but I do know, without a doubt that they *were* intimate—looks a lot like me is not a slap to the face. It is not a shock. It's a knife to the gut. A wound so deep that I know it will kill me. *Slowly*. I'm hemorrhaging here in the parking lot of the Greek Cafe next to my boyfriend's former lover in front of everyone and no one can be bothered to see that I'm bleeding out one obliterating heartbeat at a time.

It's dirty, it's messy, and it's so incredibly *painful*.

It's not an injury that I will never be able to recover from.

"Claire—" someone calls but I'm too deep in my thoughts to recognize who is speaking to me. I don't even acknowledge them until they grab me by the upper arms and shake me.

"Hey!" I shout, to no one and everyone, all the same.

"Hands off, buddy!" Emma snaps at the same time. And I look up into the kind face of Detective Cruz. He's a handsome guy, has an alpha side from what I can tell, strong jaw and stronger . . . *muscles*. But he's a man and a cop and I'm finding as of late those don't make for great romantic partners. I never should have shit where I ate. But then again, I always hoped that Wes would be different, even though I knew all along that he really wasn't.

And to top it all off, he's not *just* Wes.

I never should have let myself fall in love with him, but I just couldn't stop it. Wes has held my heart in the palm of his hand my whole life.

Something darker than concern flashes across his eyes as he looks to Emma. "I just wanted to make sure she was okay," he snaps.

"Of course, I'm okay," I say softly trying to diffuse the situation. "Why wouldn't I be?"

"Because that jackass hurt you *again!*" he roars.

"I'm fine," I say for everyone to hear. "I'm sad that another life was lost this one being one of our own. We will solve this together."

"That's it?" he asks incredulous.

"That's what?" I say feeling my frustration ramp up.

"You're just going to run right back to him after all that he's done," Cruz sneers.

"Excuse me?" How dare a fellow detective question my personal life. I'm so done with this bullshit.

They all do it. Every last one of the men in my station think that they have free reign to put their nose in my business and judge me. Or worse tattle on me to my brother like we're back on the kindergarten playground.

"Detectives?" Liam says as he approaches us. Speak of the devil himself. My day is either about to get better or it's about to go straight to hell. Lee's appearance at an active crime scene where I had to remove my boyfriend—a.k.a. his best buddy—as a suspect tells me that and more.

"Nothing," Cruz says before walking away. "Not a damn thing."

"What was that all about?" Lee asks quietly enough that only I can hear him.

"I'm not entirely sure." I shrug. "It'll all work itself out." He studies me as only a brother can. I do my best not to flinch or squirm, keeping my eyes locked on his like I used to do when I was little and I had challenged him to a staring contest.

"You okay?" he questions softly for only me to hear. "It's alright if you're not. A lot has happened."

"You, know what? I'm not. But I owe it to Tawnya to keep my shit together. For now."

"Okay," he says before turning to the crowd of officers, agents, and crime scene people. His eyes linger on Emma until her cheeks burn bright red and she looks away. Then he calls out, "Listen up people. This is one of our own. Not GWTPD, but FBI, but you and I know that we're all blue on the inside. The blood in our veins all runs the same." He pauses to take a moment to make eye contact with every officer and agent on the scene. "I want this scene spotless. I want you all to be so far above par that the investigation is perfect. Because Agent Webber deserves that. And she deserves nothing less than that. I want this fucker caught *now*!"

A cheer goes up among all of the police officers and agents. I have to admit, Liam gives a good speech. He's a great Captain—when he's not terrorizing me and my career choices, *that is*.

When the dust settles again, everyone goes back to what they were doing. Crime scene is still taking pictures and samples. Emma is instructing her people on how to prep the body for transport to her lab. The officers and agents are questioning everyone in the cafe if they saw anything out of the ordinary.

"Emma," I call out.

"Yeah?" she asks as she runs up to me effectively angling her body so that she has her back turned to Liam.

"I want that autopsy first thing in the morning," I tell her.

"You got it, boss." She mock salutes.

"But I'm the boss," Liam corrects.

"Sure, you are buddy. Sure, you are." She winks as she pats him on the chest before walking by. Lee's jaw tenses as he clenches his teeth. It appears my girl really knows how to push his buttons.

"It's nothing," he grounds out.

"Sure, sure," I say to appease my brother who is also my boss. "I didn't see anything."

"If I say it's nothing, it's nothing!" he barks.

"Okay," I say as I hold my hands out in front of me in surrender.

Five hours and no answers later, everyone is frustrated and angry.

"I can't believe no one saw a Goddamned thing!" Tawnya's partner shouts. "Are you *officers* good for anything?"

"I get that you're upset. We all are," I say keeping my voice low and my warning private. "But you cannot speak to me or my officers that way again."

"Oh yeah," he sneers leaning in, nose to nose with me. "Watch me."

"You wouldn't be threatening one of my detectives would you, Agent Procter?" Liam asks casually as he saunters up. Knowing Lee, he is anything but casual. He's about as casual as a tiger ready to strike.

The Agent laughs meanly. "Of course, you would have her back. Big brother's always do, don't they? Even though we both know that she should have been sacked years ago."

He doesn't get to say anymore because Liam punches him in the mouth.

"Did you see that?" the Agent shouts. "Look at what your Captain is so willing to do."

Liam just stands there with his arms folded across his chest and his mouth closed while he glares at the Agent.

"You just assaulted a Federal Agent, asshole. I have witnesses."

"Oh yeah?" I ask. "Who?"

"Well," he splutters before pointing to me. "You!"

"I didn't see anything."

"And those guys over there." Agent Procter points to Jones and a couple of other officers but they quickly turn away. His eyes widen with panic now that he knows that he's on a sinking ship. He's trying. I'll give him that.

"We didn't see anything," they call out.

"Yes, you did!" he shouts. "This is police corruption!"

"You clearly have an ax to grind where me and my officers are involved," Liam says. His arms are folded across his broad chest and his feet are spread wide. The look on his face is filled with a menacing challenge as he draws his brows down to stare at the angry agent. "I think you need to leave."

"Are you shitting me right now?" he seethes.

"No, I'm dead serious," Liam says, his tone eerily calm. "I think you need to leave. Now."

"Do you know who I am?" Agent Procter demands.

"Do I look like I care? Right now, I have a fresh body in the morgue that needs answers and a murder to investigate. You, Sir, are impeding both so unless you'd like to be brought in on charges of interference of a peace officer in the performance of their duties, please continue."

"You wouldn't dare."

"Try me," Liam leans in, his sharp, white teeth gleaming in the sun as he dances his dance with the angry agent one last time. The agent seems to ponder his options for a moment realizing that Lee will not back down on this instance. He's lost this round and he knows it.

"This isn't over," he snaps as he turns to walk away.

"You could have fooled me," Liam says to his back. The agent's back goes ramrod straight and he pauses in his tracks. I'm sure he's wondering if he can get away with beating Lee to a pulp. But Lee was a SEAL just as Wes was, not much has slowed him down in his advanced age of thirty-eight and it shows, so the man wisely keeps walking. But I have a feeling this won't be the last we hear from him.

Lee's phone rings, breaking the silence.

"Goodnite," he answers. "Roger that . . . I'll see if I can get to her before the desk sergeant does."

My ringing phone interrupts his conversation with the mystery caller.

"Goodnite," I answer.

"This is the desk sergeant, I have Special Agent Wesley O'Connell here in an interview room with his attorney, Detective."

"I'm sure there is a detective available to take his statement," I say coolly.

"He's asking for you."

"I'm not sure that that is appropriate," I say keeping my voice low. I'm hoping to not draw too much attention to myself as I answer the Sergeant. I place my fist of my free hand on my hip and lean forward, staring at my boots as if they will suddenly give me the answers I need, the secrets of the universe. But I feel their eyes on me anyway. I sigh and start walking in any direction to keep my thoughts private. I hope.

"Let me rephrase, he says he will only speak to you." That stops me right in my tracks. I'd like to say that Wes's cool maneuvering blindsided me, but it

doesn't. This is straight out of the Wesley O'Connell playbook.

"Fuck!" I bite out to no one in particular. "I'll be right there." I hang up and start to make my way back to my car when I hear a phone ring.

Liam answers it, "Goodnite." I don't pay much attention to him or anyone else as I make my way to the street where we parked until I realize that I don't have a car here because I rode here with Emma so I turn around and start stomping back to where she stands.

"Things aren't looking so good, brother. I think she knows now . . . willco," he says before he hangs up.

"Sooo . . ." he starts.

"Do. Not." I hold my hand out to him. "I need wheels." In the blink of an eye, Liam maneuvers me so that he is next to me and my arm is linked through his elbow as if he was a true, old fashioned gentleman. Which we all know that he is not—*Emma*, it seems, in particularly at this moment in time.

"It would be my honor to escort you back to the station, sister dear," he snickers.

"Ugh. Fine." I surrender just this once. It's so out of character for me that the words taste like ash in my mouth.

I see Liam start to open his mouth to say something to me as we make our way to the street where all of the department vehicles are parked side by side. I hold my hand up, palm out and stop him before he ever gets a chance.

"I said not one word, Lee." He snaps his jaw closed. "I need that right now. We'll see where we go from here once I wrap this case up. And listen here and listen good. I *will* wrap this case up."

Liam doesn't turn to look at me as he nods once to show me his understanding. He beeps the locks on his department vehicle and we climb in. My brother does not try to talk to me during the entire drive across town to the station. I take the time to think over what awaits me when we get there.

I can't help but think that Wes only wants to talk to me in order to prove his motivations where Agent Webber was concerned. And while part of me hates that he was intimate with her—my stomach is rolling at the thought—but it is my job to find out what happened to her and stop whoever did it. One thing I know for sure, the killer isn't Wes. I need to clear him and move on as quickly as possible.

Whether or not Wes is proving to be a good boyfriend is yet to be determined.

Lee pulls into his spot in the parking lot at the station. He turns towards me. I feel his stare heat the side of my face. He's not my brother now, he's my boss, and that's exactly what I need him to be. My Captain needs to know that I can do what needs to be done or else he'll pull me from the case. My brother, however, would punch Wes in the face and ask questions later. I don't look at him, instead I keep my gaze trained forward through the windshield until I can't take it anymore.

I close my eyes tight and take a deep breath.

"Not now, Lee," I say before taking another breath in an effort to slow my rapidly increasing heart rate. "Let's just get this done and move on."

"But what if it hurts?" he asks me in the quiet of

the car.

"Then I'll let it and then move on. Just like always," I say before pushing open my door and climbing out.

Liam follows me through the front doors of the station. It seems as if all conversations drift off into the ether, it's as if all movement comes to a complete stop in the lobby of the station. The desk sergeant motions to me raising his left hand. I look to him and nod my head.

"He's in interview three. His lawyer too."

"Thanks." I wave to the desk sergeant as I make my way to interview room three with Liam hot on my heels.

His heavy palm lands on my shoulder stopping me just as my hand lands on the handle of the door, stopping me from pulling the heavy steel panel opened.

"You don't have to do this, Claire," he says, his voice low and heavy with meaning. This here, is my brother, the man who cleaned up my skinned knees and patched my bicycle tires when we were kids. Now as adults, he still wants to protect me from all of the hurts of the world, but this time, we both know he can't. "You could just go sit in the observation room and watch. I'll take his statement. It'll be fine."

"You know that's not true, Lee." I sigh. "He said he won't talk to anyone but me. *Not even you.* So, we're going to talk. I'll get his statement and we'll move on from there."

"What if it's not the information you want?" he asks me.

"But what if it's the information that I need? For Agent Webber? Or for me?"

"What if you find out something and there's no turning back?" he presses.

"Then I put one foot in front of the other and keep moving forward. Just like the kid in that Disney movie says," I say to which Liam sighs.

"Sis."

"What?" I ask.

"We were having a moment and you just ruined it." I roll my eyes. "Are we good?"

"Yeah, Lee. We're good."

"Okay. Let's do this."

"Let's? As in us? Together?" I ask.

"Of course. He might only talk to you but this is still very much my house and you're still my sister, he knows that. So, let's do this, but we do it by the book. Everything is on the level because between you and me, IA are a bunch of dickless weasels and they would just love it if this turned into a three-ring shit show." I can't help the laugh that bubbles up from my chest.

"Okay, let's do this so the dickless weasels can't win the day!" I cheer.

I pull open the door to the interview room and the wave of pain and helplessness that spreads out from Wes's face slides the smile right off of my own. He does not say anything, just sits there with his palms flat on the steel table and watches me, studies me—my heart breaks for him and the desperation, the hopelessness that seeps from his pores.

Liam steps into the room behind me letting the door click softly closed behind him. The tension radiates out from everyone within these steel walls.

I clear my throat. "From here on out this conversation is being both monitored and recorded," I say as I flip the switch on the table to start the recording. We all know that the gallery is full of lookey loos wanting all the gossip on me and Wes.

"Wes," Lee says softly. "I have to do it."

"I know," Wes says, nodding his head in acceptance.

"You have the right to remain silent. Anything you say can and will be used against you in a court of law. You have the right to an attorney. If you cannot afford one, one will be provided for you. Do you understand these rights as they have been described to you?"

"Yes," Wes says clearly.

"Present are myself, Detective Claire Goodnite, Captain Liam Goodnite, and Agent O'Connell's counsel," I say for the sake of the recoding. "Please state your name."

"Special Agent in Charge Wesley O'Connell, FBI." His voice rings strong and true.

"And do you have counsel present with you, Agent O'Connell?"

"Yes," Wes answers at the same time an older man in a suit similar to the ones Rex Harrison wore in *My Fair Lady*, vest and all, answers as well.

"Present."

"And for the record you are, Sir?"

"Anthony Garrison of *Garrison, Garrison, Parker, & Stroop*, Counsel for Agent O'Connell."

"Thank you. Let's get started," I say looking at Wes. He looks determined yet sad. "Agent O'Connell, did you know Agent Tawnya Webber?"

"Yes."

"What was the nature of your relationship?" Wes opens his mouth to speak but his attorney interrupts his answer.

"Define the term relationship, Detective."

"Sure thing." I shrug. "How did you know Agent Webber?"

"We both work for the FBI. I am her senior agent in charge," he answers.

"Is that the extent of your knowledge of Tawnya Webber?" I ask.

"As of late." Wes calmly responds.

"And before then?" I press. He swallows.

"I knew her."

"How so?" I further press, not sure if I want the answer.

"We engaged in an after-hours affair for three months but it was years ago." Wes admits.

"How many years ago?" I need the specifics.

"Five years ago."

"Does the FBI allow relationships as such?" I press on.

"It's not encouraged, but it is allowed," Wes answers honestly.

"Did it affect your job?"

"Never." He states.

"Did the affair end amicably?"

"As much as they ever can?" He shrugs.

"Did you not want to part ways with her?"

"I did, she didn't."

"Did the breakup affect your working relationship?"

"No."

"Why did you end your affair?" I ask.

Wes looks me dead in the eyes as he answers, "She wasn't you."

"Inappropriate and not pertaining to the case, Wes," Lee interjects while I try and catch my breath.

"It's true. We—Lee and I," he says for my benefit before turning back to Liam. "Came home and built our careers. By the time I was ready for something serious with your sister she was ignoring me and avoiding me as if it was her job. It was clear that I wasn't going to make any headway any time soon so, ashamed as I am, I didn't give up my extracurricular activities. I realize now that I should have.

"One night we had wrapped up a pretty rough case—a kidnapping, but not like the Donovan's. Like hers—I was keeping it together, but I was in a bad way. Webber offered to take me to a local bar and get me drunk and I agreed. Once I was good and hammered, she offered to take me home and make me forget. I also agreed. But not to forget. As sick as it sounds, she looked just like . . .

"For a night I just wanted to pretend. I let it go on for three months. When she started voicing feelings for me, I knew that what I had done was wrong. I had to let her go. So, I did."

We all let his words weigh heavy in the room. The tale of Wes and Claire is not overly a happy one. And sad to say, it's future isn't looking so bright either. We've both done so many things we shouldn't have. So many wrong turns have been taken.

But this isn't about us. This right now is about catching a killer. I square my shoulders and straighten my spine. Everyone else follows my lead and knows that we are about to get back to the business at hand here.

"Agent O'Connell, did you murder Agent Tawnya Webber?"

"Don't answer that," his attorney chimes in.

"No," Wes answers anyway.

"Where were you at twelve o'clock this afternoon?"

"I was with you and Emma Parker in the morgue going over the autopsy reports of Tammy Campbell."

"Does the Greek Cafe or it's parking lot hold any meaning to you?" Wes looks me in the eye and clenches his mouth closed. I know he's holding back on me know. Whether for the case or his former affair I have yet to find out. "You might as well tell me."

"You don't have to answer," his attorney shares.

"Tawnya and I used to have lunch there." I tilt my head to the side because to my knowledge I've never eaten there. And then the embarrassment sears across my face. He doesn't mean me, he means her. "Once or twice, we fucked in the parking lot."

"Where were you during the time of Tammy Campbell's murder?"

"You have to know it didn't mean anything," he pleads. "Not to me. It didn't mean anything to me."

"Where were you during the time of Tammy Campbell's murder?" I repeat.

"Claire, please. It was only ever you. It was only you. I never loved anyone else."

"I'm going to ask you one more time before I conclude this interview. Where were you during the murder of Tammy Campbell?"

"I was with you, here at this station."

"Did you murder Tammy Campbell?"

"Don't answer!" Wes's attorney shouts.

"No." Wes states firmly.

"Where were you during the time of the murder of Bonnie Bradley?" I ask.

"At the club with your brother and a half dozen other officers."

"Did you know that she was a direct relative to me or to Captain Goodnite?"

"No."

"Did you murder Bonnie Bradley?"

"Don't answer!" The attorney shrieks. "Captain get your detective under control."

"Agent O'Connell was informed of his Miranda Rights, he is free to answer or not answer," Liam shares.

"No, I did not."

"Did you think that she looked like me before her death?" I ask.

"No, it never crossed my mind."

"No further questions," I say as I click off the recorder. "Don't leave town, Agent O'Connell. We'll be in touch."

"Claire, I love you! It was a long time ago. You have to believe me," he shouts as he rises up from the table and moves to follow me to the door. His attorney grabs him by the back of his arm and whispers something in Wes's ear. He looks pissed but Wes just keeps yelling. "You have to believe me."

My eyes flood and my nose stings as I look at Wes.

"The sad thing is I do. But we'll deal with that later," I say softly, hopefully for his ears only.

"No!" he shouts. "Fuck. Claire! I need you. You have to come back, Claire."

"Just let her go, man," I hear Lee say softly.

"No. I can't. You can't ask that of me."

"For now," Lee pleads. "Just let her go. For now."

I let the steel door close behind me but not before I hear Wes sob and call out my name one more time. I put one foot in front of the other and walk out of the station. Despite what it looks like, this time, I'm not running.

But I do have to clear my head. It's been a long day and I'm starving. I'm exhausted—both physically and emotionally and tomorrow I need to be at the top of my game. Tomorrow, I'm going to find a killer. I'm going to catch the piece of shit responsible for ending the lives of a stripper, a barista, and the former lover of my boyfriend because they deserve justice. Only then I can figure out what to do with me.

chapter 25

tribal drums

MY PULSE IS POUNDING in my ears like a tribal drum as I walk down the hall.

I pull in a deep breath through my nose and slowly force it out of my mouth. I do it again. And again, until the edges of my focus snap into place. Instead of waving all over like a flag in the breeze, I see a tunnel in front of me as I pass through the hall and down to the door.

I choose to push out of the side entrance instead of the front door where I know a ton of lookey loos are waiting to see the aftermath of my interview with Wes. I'm sure they're all waiting with baited breath to see an explosion or a meltdown. What will happen next? Well, stay tuned because I have no idea.

I need to get home and go over the case. It's been a long couple of days. I need to step back and look at everything from a different perspective. Why Wes? Why is Wes the central focus?

I push out the side door and the purple sky tells

me that my showdown with Wes took longer than I thought. Not to mention we were at the crime scene all afternoon. My stomach growls loudly as I palm my cell phone. I'm hungry and need a burrito, or like twenty tacos. It takes a lot of junk to fuel all of this magnificence.

I swipe the screen on my phone and dial the one number I know that I always can. The one person that will never judge me and will always try to guide me towards the right path. Or the one who will go down swinging with me if I do. It's also the number of the one person who will always pick me up when I need a lift.

"Hello?" they answer.

"I need a ride," I explain.

"I thought as much. I'll be there in five."

"Meet me at the cafe on first. I need a cup of coffee and to not be loitering here at the station."

"So I heard. See you then." And then they hang up. I put my phone in my pocket and start walking towards the little coffee shop on first. It's not the one that Tammy worked at, the one that Wes and I usually go to together.

This is the place I go when I need to be alone and off the radar.

I walk the last two blocks and pull open the door to a place where nobody knows my name. Where they see cops of all ranks and uniforms come through the doors because of its close proximity to the station. Here the coffee is poured, cash is accepted, and no questions are asked.

I stand in the back of the line behind the tired and

weary. It's clearly been a fantastic day all around. Although whisperings of a serial killer around town is enough to put anyone in the dumps. Or excite them. Some people are weird.

I shuffle forward inch by inch as each person before me orders and then grabs their paper cups with little brown coffee collars on them before shuffling off into the ether. Finally, I step up to the counter where a young woman—probably seventeen to nineteen years old—greets me with a smile that makes my stomach clench when I think of Tammy and her adorably harmless infatuation with Wes.

Wes.

How could one word, three little letters, make my heart ache so badly? The answer is easy. Behind those three little letters is eleven years of my loving him. No, that's the lie I tell myself. That I stopped loving him for awhile when his misguided attempt to protect me and provide for me what he thought that I needed was leaving me at eighteen—shortly after I had given him my heart and my innocence on a silver platter. The cold hard truth is, I have been in love with Wesley O'Connell my entire life. That is twenty-nine, almost thirty years, on this earth. And for that entire time, all *two hundred sixty-two thousand, nine hundred eighty* hours, *fifteen million, seven hundred seventy-eight thousand, eight hundred* minutes, and *nine hundred forty-eight million, seven hundred twenty-eight thousand* seconds of it I have been in his orbit.

The look on my face must have forced her—Emmy, her name tag says Emmy—to take a step back with wide eyes. Her smile turning just a little bit brittle around the corners of her mouth. I turn up the wattage on my own smile thinking that clearly my resting bitch face got the best of us both. *Oopsie Whoopsies.*

"Hi there. What can I get for you?"

"Just a coffee. Black," I answer before noticing the tightening of the corners of her mouth. She's clearly not impressed with my two-dollar coffee order and I can't help but find her assessment of me startling. So, I scramble to add more to my order. "Umm . . . with room for cream. Lots of room. And one of those big oatmeal raisin cookies."

"Sure thing," she says softly as she reaches over to bag my cookie. "That'll be six dollars and seventy-eight cents please."

I pull a ten-dollar bill out of my pocket and hand it to Emmy. "Thanks," I say as I take my cup and paper bag filled with a cookie that will probably taste like ash in my mouth due to all the stress I'm under.

She gives me a reproachful glare and I drop all of the change she just handed me into the tip jar. Her face instantly morphs into a look of pure delight as her new financial boon registers.

"Thank you! Come again. Anytime!"

I back away slowly and head towards the cream and sugar counter. I take the lid off my paper cup and pour a shit ton of creamer in. I chance a look over my shoulder and see Emmy watching me with an arched brow so I pour a little more in before replacing the lid and pushing out through the glass doors.

The bells chime and the sun is bright as it's setting behind the trees. I take a deep breath and shake off the mental shackles that Emmy and her teenage judgement put me in, instantly feeling silly for feeling that way. Just then Anna rolls up on what feels like two wheels in her Merc.

"Get in, loser. We're going shopping." Always with the *Mean Girls* references. For as level headed and rational that Anna is, *Mean Girls* is her Achilles Heel. The thought makes me smile.

I pull open the door and hop inside.

"Thanks for the lift, A."

"So why aren't we with the man friend?" she asks.

"What?" I volley back. "I can't call my dearest friend?"

"Save it." She shoots me a side eyed glare. "Emma called me. I know what went down at the crime scene earlier."

I sigh. "Then what are you asking me for? Clearly, you already know everything."

"She also told me that he said he would only speak to you to give his statement." She widens her eyes expressively.

"Your face is going to freeze like that." It's petty and childish I know, but currently I can't seem to help myself.

"I'm assuming that did not go well and that is why you needed me to help you execute an escape plan."

"Maybe we shouldn't bandie about the word *execute* right now."

"Stop prevaricating," she challenges.

"I don't know what you're talking about," I say folding my arms across my chest.

"Don't be petty, it doesn't become you."

"Yes, it does."

"Okay it does but stop it because I don't like it."

"Fine," I pout.

"Besides," she starts with a Cheshire Cat grin that I know for a fact means trouble. "Emma is meeting us at your place so we can both pin you down and torture all the details out of you."

I sigh. I'm well and truly fucked now.

chapter 26

grownup

THE DRIVE FROM THE little coffee shop to my apartment is silent.

Anna isn't one to fill the void with useless chatter and I can already tell that she's saving up her lecture for when she has backup. If Anna is anything, she is a planner. Anna is calm, cool, and collected. *Rational*.

Emma, on the other hand, flies by the seat of her pants. Emma operates solely on emotion and instinct. She acts first and thinks later. If she were in this car with me she would be all over me like a cheap suit. Thankfully she's not.

This gives me a moment to think up an excuse for why I cannot tell them all the gory details of my romantic life as they seem to be intersecting with my case right now. And as my dad would say, what a cluster fuck. That's actually one of my most favorite phrases as it just seems to sum things up so well. Although I never seem to have an actual reason to apply it. But with this case already running me ragged, with murder victims dressed like creepy little dolls coming out of my ears and snakes popping up at inopportune moments—I shudder at the thought—even I couldn't dream up a scenario where one of the victims had a romantic history with Wes.

It can't really be as bad as it seems. I want to tell myself that everything will work out the way that it is supposed to. That I can clear Wes's name and find the killer. And if Lady Luck is really on my side, I can repair the relationship that I wasn't even sure that I wanted until recently. All while avoiding Emma and Anna's inquisition like a long-tailed cat in a house full of *River Dancers*. Who am I kidding? I am well and truly screwed. I might as well just tell them what they want to know.

She pulls the Merc into a spot just in front of the stairs as if it had been waiting for her to drive up all along. Ugh. I groan. How does she have all the luck? In all the years that I have lived here I have never been lucky enough to nab this space.

Anna turns to look at me when that terrible noise crawled up from my throat and rolls her eyes. I'm assuming that she mistakes my groan for not wanting to be ambushed and tortured by my two closest friends instead of envy of her ridiculous parking karma.

"Come on," she says softly. "Let's just get this over with."

"Okay."

She turns, unbuckling her seatbelt and pushing her door open. Anna climbs from her Merc with the grace of a ballet dancer. She works so closely with the department sometimes that I forget that she isn't really one of us, the rougher crowd that can seamlessly mingle with the city's underbelly to root out the answers we need. Anna, is a trust fund baby who went to an Ivy League school—Princeton! It's moments like this when she lets the mask slip for a second, she's pushing her door open and climbing the stairs to my place with a look of sadness in her eyes that she doesn't usually show to the world. I wonder what a weight this life is on her, what toll does it really take from her, when I see her like this.

"Christ, Claire, hurry up," she shouts at me. "Christmas is coming!"

And then, when she turns back to me, I see that that look, is gone. So, I brush off those feelings, the maudlin thoughts that can weigh any of us down from time to time, and I follow her up the stairs. Emma throws open my front door when Anna and I reach the landing.

"Fucking hell! It took you long enough. I'm dying here. Literally. Dying."

Anna rolls her eyes. "You're not literally dying or you would, in fact, be dying right now."

"Shut it, Fancy Pants. She knows what I mean."

"I'm just saying . . ." she grumbles. I can't help but laugh.

"And you!" Emma wheels on me. I hold my hands up in surrender.

"I'm starving," I say quickly changing the subject. Sort of. "I need sustenance before you interrogate me."

"Ugh. Fine," Emma shouts, throwing her hands up over her head as she makes her way over to my refrigerator. She pulls open the door and stops in her tracks. "You have got to be kidding me."

"What?" I ask feeling a little offended at her reaction to the contents of my fridge.

"There's like an old container of eel sauce in here that smells like used cat litter and a quart of milk so curdled it's cottage cheese from hell. How do you live like this?"

"Like what?" I ask.

"Like . . . like a toddler or a frat boy."

"That's ridiculous," I complain.

"Is it really?" Anna chimes in.

"Yes!" I say.

"No!" Emma volleys back.

"Ugh!" I grumble throwing my hands up like ET over my head. "I am a grown up!"

"You could have fooled me," Emma mumbles.

"What was that?" I snap. I'm spoiling for a fight. At this point, I'll do anything to keep them from asking me the hard questions, even if that means a knock down drag out with one of my best friends.

"Look," Anna tries for diplomacy. "Let's just order delivery. What does everyone feel like?"

"Chinese," I answer immediately. Both Anna and Emma stare silently with their jaws hanging open. "What?" I ask after a moment of awkwardness.

"Ch-Chinese?" Anna asks after clearing her throat.

"Yeah, why?"

"Really?" Emma asks.

"Really." I nod.

"But you were poisoned with Chinese food!" Emma shouts.

"Oh!" I say realizing what they were talking about. "That was ages ago. I love Chinese food." Emma closes her eyes and shakes her head side to side rapidly, almost like she's trying to clear an Etch-a-sketch.

"Oh-kay . . ." Anna agrees.

"Great!" I cheer excitedly. Chinese food really perks me right up. "I have a menu right here." I pull open one of the kitchen drawers and start rooting through all of the take-out menus."

"Sweet Christ!" Emma barks. "There must be menus for every restaurant in the tri-city area." She does not seem nearly as impressed about that as I am.

"I know. It took me a long time to collect them all." I finally find the one that I want and hold it up like the monkey holds the baby lion in the beginning of *the Lion King*. Emahama emee momabah! "Got it!"

"What was that you were saying about being a grown up?" Anna drolls.

"Shut up!" I snap. "You want food or not?"

"Mu-shu chicken please." She bats her pretty blue eyes at me.

"You're lucky you're so pretty," I say as I slide my finger across the screen of my phone to unlock it. I press the number one speed dial setting to connect with my favorite Chinese place.

"I'm not even going to comment on the fact that you have a take-out place as the number one speed dial in your phone . . ." Emma rolls her eyes.

"Even before us?" Anna asks sounding just a little appalled as the phone rings.

I nod my head yes. "Don't worry your pretty little heads." I smile evilly. "It's also ahead of Wes and the station."

The line connects. "Hello and thank you for calling Szechuan Palace. How may we help you?"

"Hi, Mr. Yao," I answer.

"Claire! So good to hear from you. The usual?"

"Of course. And another order of Mu-Shu Chicken and an order of Beef with Broccoli please." I wink at Emma just to rile her up.

"So . . ." Anna says breaking the silence as we all poke at our take-out containers with chopsticks. "How about them, Yankees?"

"What the fuck are you talking about?" I ask.

"Wes." She nods. I groan.

"I mean, you did walk right into that one," Emma adds cheerfully. "I'm surprised the good head doctor didn't just come right out and say it."

"What's that supposed to mean?" Anna asks clearly a little offended at the head doctor comment.

"Don't get your panties in a wad, Fancy Pants. I just meant that you're usually more direct than this."

"Well . . ." she hedges. "I was just trying to be a little considerate of Claire's feelings."

"It's alright, Anna," I say softly. "You may proceed with your interrogation."

"Thank you," she says politely before rolling her shoulders back and carrying on with her intended mission. "Emma said that Wes knew the Agent that was killed today."

"Ha!" Emma snarks. "Knew her, he was banging her."

"Presently?" Anna asks.

"No," I answer, my voice still quiet.

"Are you sure?" Emma asks.

"He says so."

"Do you feel like you can trust the veracity of his claims?" Anna asks not at all unkindly, just . . . interested. She's evaluating the situation.

I sigh before standing up. "I was wrong. We're going to need my boyfriend for this conversation."

"Boyfriend?" Emma and Anna ask in unison.

"I believe you might know him as Gentleman Jack."

"Ahh." Anna nods.

I grab the bottle from the top shelf in my little kitchen. I unscrew the cap and take a heavy swig straight from the bottle.

"Classy as always." Emma winks before reaching for the bottle. She belts back a sip before handing it to Anna.

Anna takes her own swig before coughing. Emma pats her on the back hard. "God, that's truly terrible."

"Hush your mouth! You might hurt his feel bads." I laugh.

She rolls her eyes at me. "Quit evading the question."

I shrug. "I'm not evading, I just thought this conversation would be more bearable if we were shit faced." I take another swig from the bottle before passing it on and picking up my take-out container.

"That's such a hideous turn of phrase." Anna laughs before taking another hit from the bottle. "It does become more manageable the more you drink it."

Emma and I both snicker.

"Now answer the question Fancy Pants asked you."

Emma urges.

I sigh. "I do trust him. Wes that is."

"Okay," Anna says taking a deep breath after another sip. "What happened at the scene?"

"Agent Webber's partner was upset and rubbed my nose in the affair that everyone knew about but me."

"And how did that make you feel?"

"Shitty," I answer. "How would you feel?"

"Not good," she says after a pause. I look to Emma to see if she knows what's up with our favorite shrink but her face is purposely blank.

"It was not good." I take a deep breath and prepare myself to spill it all to my two closest friends whether or not I want to. "Wes had to leave the scene because it's now a conflict of interest."

"How do you feel about that?" Anna questioned.

"It is a conflict of interest. I would rather Wes recuse himself to be cleared by a third party than have him muddy the waters by being a dumbass."

"Fair enough," Emma adds.

"Then Lee basically threw down with her partner," I add.

"What?" Anna asks, her back going straight. I barely had time to register how Emma bristled at the mention of my brother's name. Something is going on here.

"He kept bad mouthing me and the department in front of everyone working the scene. Lee sent him packing but it almost came to blows." I explain.

"That's terrible," she breathes.

"I'm sure Captain Goodnite can handle himself just fine." Emma snorts before she realizes what she said and her fair face turns beet red.

"What is going on between you and Lee?" I ask unfortunately before I see Anna's flinch. Oh shit. I thought she was over her crush.

Emma looks pointedly at Anna while answering my question. "Not one Goddamned thing."

"Fair enough," I say.

Anna rolls her shoulders back before pressing on. "What happened after Liam—*Captain Goodnite*— turned the agent away?" She quickly corrects herself.

"We worked the scene. It was the same old, same old, and then Emma hauled her away in her mondo body mover." I shrug.

"Not so fast there," Emma wades in. "Let's back up the old Sioux canoe here."

"I'm not sure I know what you mean . . ." I hedge.

"Of course, you do," Emma says looking me straight in the eyes and calling out my bold-faced lie before turning to Anna. "Agent Webber had an uncanny resemblance to our singing squaw over here," she says to Anna while tossing her thumb over her shoulder at me.

"I wouldn't say we look that similar . . ."

Emma shoots me a withering glare. "She could have been your sister."

"I mean . . . not really."

"Wasn't Bonnie Bradley actually your sister?" Anna asks quietly.

"Umm . . ." I mentally grapple for any answer that doesn't seem as bad as it is.

"That's what I thought." Emma sits back folding her arms across her chest.

"What are you thinking?" Anna asks.

I blow out a breath. "That it's kind of messed up that Wes was with someone for so long that looked like me. Just because she was available and happened to look like me."

"That doesn't sound good," Anna says before biting her lip, a sure sign that she is not sure of the situation.

"It's not." I shrug. "It is what it is. There's no putting the toothpaste back in the tube on this one. I guess what it really comes down to is how much do I love him?"

"And do you?" Anna asks. "Love him?"

I take another sip from the now almost empty bottle. "I do."

"Alright then. What happened next?" Anna presses on.

"The desk sergeant called and told me Wes was at the station to give his official statement."

"That's it?" she asks to which Emma snickers.

"Oh no, it's not." She giggles. Emma is clearly a little intoxicated. But then again, so am I.

"He said he would only talk to me," I spit the words out as fast as I can.

"Oh fuck," Anna says.

"You got that right," Emma agrees.

"Then what happened?"

"He told me all the dirty details of his affair with Agent Webber and promised that he didn't kill her."

"And then what?"

"I left the interview room."

"And Wes just let you go?" she asks confused and I

can see why. From the moment Wes re-entered my life eight months ago he had made his intentions towards me crystal fucking clear. So, for him to just let me go seems a little anticlimactic.

"Not really . . ." I hesitate.

"Did you fight?" Emma asks.

"No." I sigh. "There was nothing more to talk about and I knew that everyone and their mother in that station was piled up high on the observation deck. So, I left to go recharge my batteries and regroup. That's when I called Anna."

"But he just let you go?" Emma asks.

"No. He was screaming my name. He was with Lee the last time I saw him. But I have to solve this case and to do that I have to clear him of any wrongdoing aside from the affair. I can't do that clean with him so closely connected to me. It has to be by the book."

"I can see where you're coming from . . ." Anna hedges.

"Maybe you should call him," Emma jumps in.

"I can't. I can't show any conflict of interest or ma-nipulation of the case or the FBI will rip it right out from underneath me." I take the bottle from Emma and take a long sip. "I'm close. I know it. I'm so close to figuring it all out that I can feel it."

"Well." Emma sighs. "There's nothing more we can do tonight. Especially while I'm this drunk. I will have the lab reports back on Agent Webber in the morning so let's just decompress tonight."

"Sounds like a plan," I agree. "Movie?"

"Yes!" Anna cheers. Clearly excited for a girls' night.

I push myself up off the couch and sway just a teensy tiny bit before walking down the hall to my bedroom. I change into a pair of pajama shorts and a tank before grabbing some clean pajamas out of the dresser drawer and heading back to the living room.

"Here you bitches go," I say as I toss the content towards their faces. I squint in an effort to make them fly in the direction I was hoping for.

I toss my hair up into a messy bun on top of my head and sit—and by sit, I mean flop unceremoniously—on the floor by the sofa and pick my take out back up. Emma and Anna take turns changing in my little bathroom before we all sit back down.

"Anyone want a microwave warm up?" I ask as Anna flips through the channels on the TV. There's a chick flick movie marathon on one of the local channels. Hooray. I don't think we could handle anything bloodier than a broken heart right now.

"Nah," Emma says. "I kind of prefer Chinese food cold."

"Amen to that!" Anna cheers. She's cute when she's tipsy. I just wish she wasn't headed towards a heartbreak from my dipshit brother. He can be such an asshole sometimes.

We settle in and relax. Emma was right, there's nothing we can do now. I only hope that Wes knows that while I can't contact him, he needs to trust me. It will all work out tomorrow.

"This just in . . ." the TV station cuts to the local news. *"We're here with breaking news as it appears a Serial Killer is on the loose in George Washington Township."*

"You have got to be kidding me," I growl as I turn up the volume on the set.

"This station received a tip from a credible law enforcement source who wishes to remain nameless . . ."

"I'll just fucking bet he does. I'll have his badge for this," I growl.

"That's if you can prove it," Emma says. "I bet that fucker covered his tracks."

"Our source claims that George Washington Township PD has been keeping valuable information away from the public. Information that could very well keep you safe at night. And those responsible for withholding the truth are none other than Captain Liam Goodnite and Detective Claire Goodnite . . .", I groan.

"You all will remember Detective Goodnite, who graced headlines during the high-profile kidnapping of a six-year-old boy, Anthony Donovan. This is the same detective who was abducted herself at six years old. That case is still unsolved."

"That's right, Cynthia. In fact, some George Washington residents wonder how fit she is to actually be a police officer in this district. In fact, some have said that she only holds the job because her brother is Captain Liam Goodnite. Not to mention their father is retired Chief of Police Adam Goodnite."

"I bet those are fun family dinners."

"I'm going to shoot them." I seethe.

"Now Claire, you can't threaten to shoot the public," Anna says softly whill giving me the side eye.

"Watch me."

"Not to mention Detective Goodnite has been linked romantically to Special Agent Wesley O'Connell.

That's Judge O'Connell's son to you."

"That would be the same Agent O'Connell who our source tells us was being interrogated at the precinct this afternoon." I groan.

"No, I'm not going to shoot them. I'm going to shoot that fucking fed!" I yell.

"We have it on good authority that all three victims of this serial killer were dressed and posed like old fashioned dolls."

"That mother fucker is releasing closed details of this case!" I seethe.

"It's all rather disturbing. Am I right, Ted?"

"They won't go there, right?" Emma asks. Me? I'm not so sure.

"Surly not," Anna agrees. I'm still not holding my breath. I've been thrown under this bus before so I recognize the beep-beep as it heads my way.

"Absolutely. In fact, we're told that all of the victims have been linked to Agent O'Connell. So, the question remains, is Detective Goodnite too close to the case? Will these poor women ever find justice or will the GWTPD cover up for the true killer?"

"Omigod," Anna whispers.

"Fuck me, they went there." Emma agrees.

"I guess we'll just have to stay tuned . . ."

"I'm going to go to bed," I say quietly. Even to me, my voice sounds toneless, dead.

"Everything will look better in the morning, Claire," Anna tells me.

"She's right," Emma says.

"Sure," I agree. "I'll see you both in the morning. It'll all be better in the morning."

Too bad in the morning we'd all find out just how wrong we were.

chapter 27

results are in

R^{UN!} *I'm running as fast as my little feet will take me through the woods behind my parents' house. I have to get away from the bad man. If he catches me now, I'll never get away. I have to be free.*

Run! I have to run faster.

I see the blue gray light as it spills through the trees. Mommy always told me this was her favorite part of the day—looking at the sun as it comes up in the morning. I ran away late in the night when the bad man was sleeping. It was my only chance. After he broke the lock on the closet door I knew that I had a chance to get out.

Free.

I'm free. That's the words in my head as the trees break and I see Wes standing at the edge of the back-yard. I'm free. I'm finally free. Wes looks up and he sees me.

"I've got her!" he shouts to someone.

My heart is beating so hard in my chest and it hurts to breathe. I'm so tired but I have to keep running. I see Wes, his face, I know that he'll protect me. Wes always protects me. He will keep me safe. He will keep me free.

I push my feet just a little harder, I run just a little faster. I'm almost there. I'm almost free when a strong hand wraps around my arm so hard that it hurts, pulling me around to face him, not Wes, the bad man. Wes is gone and the only person near me is the man I would do anything to get away from.

"No!" I scream.

"You're mine, Claire. You'll never be free."

Beep . . . beep . . . beep . . .

My alarm blares on the table next to my bed. A bed which in the cold light of day seems unrealistically huge and cold without Wes's body in it next to mine. Somewhere along the way, I got used to his presence in my bed, in my life, and in my heart.

I squeeze my eyes closed. That bright morning light is like ice picks in my occipital sockets. Oh, a gentleman you were not, Jack. My head is pounding with the beat of my heart and it feels like my mouth is stuffed with cotton. I halfway think I might have died last night and no one told me yet.

Coffee. I need some fucking coffee.

I peel the covers back and gingerly push my body to sitting. I have to bury my face in my hands to stop the room from spinning. So far, not so good. I swallow back the bile that pools in my mouth and force myself to stand. I press my brain to try and see his face, a tattoo, a scar, anything, but just my luck, to me the bad man is still a blur.

I push myself to my feet and instantly regret it. The combination of the Jack and the nightmare have me running for the bathroom. I barely make it, dropping to my knees in front of the toilet before emptying my stomach of its contents. Sweat mats the baby hairs to the back of my neck and my forehead. I wipe my mouth with a piece of toilet paper before dropping it in and hitting the handle.

More slowly this time, I rise to my feet and rinse my mouth out at the sink. Now I really do need some coffee. I walk out into the kitchen and find Emma and Anna gone but a note on the counter.

C,

We look like shit and headed home. Jack is a real dick. I'm considering a breakup. Nah, who am I kidding? He'll be my hot date this weekend. I'll see you at the station don't forget, the results are in.

Oh, and we made coffee. You're fucking welcome.

Xo, Emma (Anna too but with less curse words)

The note makes me smile. Those two are ridiculous and I love them. Who would have thought my besties would be a chick who likes to put her hands in dead bodies and my shrink? Not me.

I move to the counter where blessedly—praise Jesus and all the baby angels—a fully loaded coffee pot is waiting for me. I pull a mug down and pour the steaming liquid into my cup. I don't even replace the carafe, I just hold it in one hand while the other hand raises my full mug to my lips and I gulp half of it down hot and black before refilling the cup. I drink the next cup with cold leftover Chinese food as a chaser. Perfect cure for a hangover.

I take my mug into the bathroom with me and turn the water on. I keep it icy instead of letting it heat up because my body still feels too hot and sticky. The coffee isn't helping matters either but it's a necessity at this juncture.

I strip off my clothes and step in letting out a hiss as the cool spray lands on my back. I make quick work of my shower because I have important shit to do today and standing here letting my nightmares take me back down isn't one of them. Somewhere halfway through my brisk scrubbing, I reach a hand out of the shower and grab my mug off of the counter. I drain it before setting it down on the shower floor—where I'll forget it as soon as it's there.

I turn off the water and grab my towel off of the rack. It's old and worn and rough to the skin. It's nothing like the fancy shit Wes keeps at his house. Maybe I'm not as much of a grown up as I had originally thought.

I follow my earlier path back into the bedroom and through to my closet where I pull on panties and a bra. My favorite jeans and t-shirt come next and then my boots. I grab my gun and holster from the bedside table and clip them on. My badge follows. I grab my drop gun and ankle holster from the safe and check the rounds before inserting them in my boot.

I grab my keys and cellphone before heading out the door only to find that my car is still in Wes's driveway. Today is really frustrating. I pull out my phone and open the find-a-friend app. I click all the buttons to see where Wes is and find that he's at Lee's house on the opposite end of town from his own home which sits in the same quiet neighborhood as our parents have always lived.

I close out that app and order an Uber to Wes's house. Just what I need to start my day, a walk of shame slink away from my boyfriend's house. What can I say? My life is magical.

A white dodge neon that's missing all of the paneling on one side pulls up and rolls down the window.

"You Claire?" he asks.

"Yeah."

"Get in." I do as I'm told and pull open the rear door, climbing in. The entire inside reeks of pot. Classy dude. He eyes me in the rearview mirror and sweat starts to bead on his forehead. "You a cop?"

"Yep." I pop the *p* in my response to let him sweat a little more.

"You making me drive myself to jail?"

"Nope."

"You making me drive you to another cop's house?"

"No." I smile my sweetest smile at him in the mirror. "A Fed's."

"What?"

"It's okay, I'm going to steal my car back, not bust you for a little Mary Jane."

He takes an audible breath. "Thanks, lady."

"No prob, Bob." And then he drove me to my boyfriend, the Fed in questions' house, so that I could steal my car back.

Once in the driveway, I step out of the car. "Thanks, bud—" I start to say but before I can close the door, let alone finish that sentence, he's peeling out. I shrug. He seemed like a nice kid. I snicker to myself at the thought.

And then I realize I'm loitering around a Fed's house in the early morning hours. A Fed I am not supposed to be hanging around. Plus, if he comes back and catches me, I'll have to explain myself and then we'll all be in a pickle because I won't be on the case anymore. That will probably really piss me off.

This is when I enact my very best *Charlie's Angels* maneuvers. I creep around the building to the driveway on the far side of the house. I press the unlock button on the key fob and jump a mile when the locks beep. Jesus Christ it's like I forgot all of my training.

I sigh to myself and then jump into the driver's seat. I crank the ignition as fast as I can and put the pedal to the metal and head for the station. I need to go over all of the case details again. I wasn't kidding when I told my friends that I could feel how close I was. I know that the killer is out there. And I know that he's close. I just have to figure it out before anyone else gets killed or Wes gets thrown in the old hoosegow. That would really be a bummer.

chapter 28

find out

LIKE A DOG WITH a bone. That's what my dad always said about me when I had to find out the answers to whatever questions were plaguing my mind. He would also tell you that's what makes me a decent detective.

Liam would tell you that it just makes me a pain in the ass. Wes, I'm not so sure. I just hope he can hang tight a little longer. Just a tiny bit longer.

I pull into the parking lot and take the first available space I see regardless of whether or not it's in the back of the lot. I don't care. I grab my keys from the ignition and jump down from my Tahoe, slamming the door closed behind me. I'm running as soon as my boots touch the ground.

Running. Just like in my dream, I'm running.

I slow my pace just in time to avoid hitting the glass doors as they pushed open and Detective Cruz walks out.

"Good morning, Claire," he says to me with a

sweet smile.

"Hey," I say. I'm trying my best to avoid talking to anyone. Not because I'm that anti-social, well, I am, but I need to get down to the basement and talk to Emma. She promised me results and I want them.

"Where's the fire?" He asks.

"I have to get to the morgue," I explain as I move past him. "Emma promised me results."

"Gotcha. Feel like grabbing a pizza later?" His harmless question stops me in my tracks and I turn to look back at him. I tip my head to the side and study him a bit before answering.

"I can't," I say softly hoping against hope that I haven't hurt his feelings. We do have to work together for all time.

"Sure," he says but his tone is weird. Maybe this is the last time he'll ask me out. Maybe I'll regret it later if—or when—Wes and I explode into a fiery blaze of not glory but until then, I'm a little relieved. It's hard being a nice person, all considerate of people's feelings and shit. I should just go back to being a bitch.

I push through the doors without ever looking back and hot foot it to the elevator. I jab the call button again and again hoping it will make the elevator come faster. A couple of detectives walk over to where I'm standing in the elevator bay and look as if they are about to push the call button. I shoot them a dark glare and they immediately change directions and head for the stairs.

Good fucking choice, assholes.

The elevator announces its arrival with a ding. Finally! I hop in and stab the button for the basement morgue with my finger. Thankfully, the steel cart deposits me in the basement without stops.

"Fucking finally!" Emma shots and then winces. Clearly, she's feeling about as spectacular as I am this morning.

She stalks over to her desk in the corner like a hungry lioness and rips open the drawer. Emma pulls out a massive bottle of ibuprofen and shakes out what has to be an unhealthy amount of little white tablets into her hand before tossing them all into her mouth. I cringe when I hear her crunching them between her teeth before she swallows down a cup of coffee on her desk like a hooker on a first date.

"Want some?" She shakes the bottle at me. We both jolt at the rattling sound the pills make in the bottle.

"No, thanks. I'm good."

She shrugs. "Suit yourself."

"So, what do you have?" I ask.

"Well, the results are in."

"And?" I can barely stand it. Something is about to give way. I just know it.

"Agent Webber's death is exactly the same as the others right down to the handmade old timey dress and the creepy sleeping pose."

"Tox screen?"

"Benzene injected right between the neck and shoulder. Would have rendered her totally paralyzed within minutes."

"Did you do a rape kit?" I ask feeling my excitement build.

"What? Are you new here?" Emma snaps. Someone is not a happy camper this early in the morning after a night out with Gentleman Jack.

"No, I'm not new here, asshole. But I do need all the details and quick."

"She was raped. But wait for it, no condom lubricant was found in the vaginal cavity. No DNA was found on her body. Semen was present and accounted for."

"You're kidding me. He left DNA?" I ask.

"DNA that is currently being run through CODIS," she tells me. I blow out a breath of frustration. The hardest part of this job is being patient when you want action. Liam always described his time in the military as *hurry up and wait* and that's exactly what case work feels like.

"This is the mistake I was waiting for him to make." I state.

"This is the mistake, you were waiting for him to make," Emma repeats.

"Cause of death?" I ask but I already know.

"Strangulation."

"Overall, it's creepy as hell," I add.

"It really is." She nods and then closes her eyes. Clearly the fist full of pills didn't completely take away her hangover.

"Where is the benzene coming from? It can't be that easy to get."

"Actually, it really is," she answers. "Benzene is a man-made chemical used in a lot of different business-es. It's used in rubbers, plastics, pesticides, detergents, drugs, explosives. You can even buy it online from one of those websites where they ship it to you in two days in a little brown box."

"Ugh. This is so frustrating!" I shout as I pull at

my hair which I left loose this morning because the thought of pulling it up had my still pounding head screaming.

"We'll figure it out," she says softly from behind me. "I emailed you the report."

"Thanks, Em." I sigh. I'm going to go upstairs to the conference room and go over all of the case details."

"Let's grab some disgusting cheeseburgers or greasy pizza around noon to break this hangover."

"Sounds good to me," I say as I toss a wave over my head as I head back to the elevator. But as sick as I feel, I still have too much pent up energy over this case so I bypass the elevator and push open the door to the stairwell. I take the stairs two at a time.

I make my way to my desk where I boot up and log into my geriatric computer from the stone age. The department resources are stretched ever so thin. I kind of want to call up those news anchors from last night and be like see this computer that is older than me? Clearly, I am getting all the favors being the Captain's little sister. I roll my eyes but the action rattles something loose in my brain.

I log into the department server and pull the reports that Emma had sent me. She's pretty meticulous about her autopsy reports and making sure all of her i's are dotted and her t's are crossed. It makes it easy for us to pull the pertinent information from her doctor speak.

I send the files I need to the printer at the back of the bullpen. I could go stand over another one of the dinosaurs in this office while it takes four hundred years to print or I could go grab another cup of coffee from the kitchenette. I choose the coffee.

I bump into Jones who is also pouring himself a cup in the kitchen area.

"Hey there, Detective." He smiles at me.

"Hey, Jones. How's the wedding planning going?" I ask.

"Great. My girl says she bought her dress so we're all locked and loaded."

"That is great," I agree.

"Will we see you and O'Connell there?" he asks me before squeezing his eyes tight and biting his lip in obvious regret for asking the question. I shoot him my most genuine smile. "I'm sorry. That was insensitive."

"It's okay," I reassure him. "I'm sure everything will blow over by the big event."

"You're probably right, Detective." Jones takes his cup of coffee before heading back out.

I step up to the coffee maker and pour myself another cup. Station coffee is usually so thick it's a caffeinated pudding you can eat with a spoon. So, I doctor it with as much cream and sugar as I can find before heading out to the massive dinosaur printer which is wheezing like a ninety-eight-year-old lady with emphysema. It probably does have emphysema. It sounds like it could keel over and go tits up at any moment.

I stand there and watch it spit out the last of my reports as I sip my cup of coffee. When the last pages struggle to slip free, I grab them all up in my arms and head for the conference room that has become my battle station ever since this case turned from one creepy murder to a serial killer that has me trapped in an epic game of cat and mouse. I only hope he knows that I'm not the mouse. I'm a fucking lioness.

I spread out the reports in front of me: Bonnie, Tammy, and Tawnya. I match up all of the same details. I make notes of what links the three of them all together. But still, all arrows point to Wes and I know that it has to be a false lead. I just know it.

At noon, Emma comes to get me and as promised, we head to a burger joint around the corner. We each order giant burgers on buttery buns with fries and vanilla milkshakes. We bypass the vegetable station after we pick them up, opting for the nacho cheese dispenser. Grease is not only the word, but also the ultimate hangover cure. And who knows? Maybe it will shake something loose that's been lodged in my brain and everything will make sense.

"What's got you so down?" She asks me.

"I just can't find the real lead that I need. By all accounts, every detail points to Wes."

"How so?" she asks me.

"Well, Agent Webber, obviously. But also, Tammy had a huge crush on him. We went to that coffee shop almost every morning on our way to work."

"Okay, but what about the first victim?" Emma asks before taking a huge bite of the cheese covered burger. "What's the connection there?"

"He was at Jones's bachelor party at the strip club."

"Those connections are week, babe," she says after taking a sip of her drink. I bite into my burger and mull over her words. "There were tons of people at the strip club that night, not just Wes. And he wouldn't have sent you pictures with the intent to incriminate himself."

"That's true," I agree.

"In fact, half of our station was at the strip club that night for Jones's party," she says calmly. "And only about a billion people go to that coffee shop because it's more personable than the other one near the station. You know, the one you had Anna pick your bum ass up from yesterday after you made your grand exit—stage left."

"Shut up," I grumble as I dip a fry in a big blob of orange cheese goo in my basket and swirl it around before popping it into my mouth.

"So really, it could be a number of people including someone who works at or near the station."

"There's no way an officer in our station would do those things," I say with a confidence in my voice that I'm not quite sure that I feel. But could she be right? Could it really be as easy as all that?

"Sure," she says but as I look up I realize maybe Emma doesn't really feel very sure of that statement either.

Emma and I walked back to the station in silence after we finished our lunches. I couldn't help but think about all that she had said over lunch. Maybe I'm missing something simple. As I go to push open the glass door at the front of the station, Emma stops me by placing her hand on my arm.

"It'll all be okay," she says softly and it startles me. Emma is bold and brash. Soft isn't necessarily a word that I would use to describe her. But in this moment, it does. There's something going on with Emma and I can't quite figure out what it is.

"Sure," I say back just as softly.

"I mean it, Claire. It has to . . . it has to work out for you and Wes. It just does," she says before pushing open the front door and heading straight to the elevator. Something is definitely off with Emma. When this case is over, I'm going to have to get to the bottom of it.

Emma's words tumble over and over in my brain and I can't seem to shake them. I just can't make heads or tails of this investigation.

I spend the rest of the afternoon not pouring over the details of the case, but the lists if officers, detectives, and federal agents who were present at each crime scene. The fact of the matter is that the same names keep popping up over and over again. What if what Emma said is right?

Holy shit it's someone from this department.

I stand before I even realize that I'm doing it. I gather up as many of the papers as I can. Suddenly I need to be anywhere but in this station house. I need to go home and be alone. I need to wrap my mind around the idea that someone I know, that someone I work with every day could, in fact, be a serial killer.

Who could be the wolf in sheep's clothing?

I scoop up my messy stack of papers in my arms and hustle out the door. I practically run through the bullpen and then out the front door of the station—not even bothering to wave hello or goodbye to the desk sergeant on my way out even though he called out my name.

Instead I beep the locks on my department Tahoe and climb in like my hair is on fire. I start up the engine on the only piece of department equipment in my possession that isn't four hundred years old—even my service weapon is probably from the first world war—and race for my apartment like my life depends on it because if I'm right, it does.

They think they're so smart.

Everyone thinks they are so smart but I'm about to show them how brilliant I really am. They think they know, they don't know. I can't help but laugh at the thought that the world think's that stupid Fed is behind all the murders.

Part of me wishes I could take credit for all of my work. Part of me yearns for the world to know how much planning and hard work goes into my master pieces. That I had sewn each of those dresses late at night and first thing in the morning before heading to work. That I wanted to make those women perfect, just like her. But they'll never be perfect.

She's going to be my final piece here—my last hurrah before I move on—and I always move on. A new name in a new town and a new project. Let's be real, a new . . . obsession. I have obsessed over her for months and still she doesn't see my devotion! I had thought she would be the one to stop the compulsion to kill. That her perfection would curb the desire but in the end, she isn't as perfect as I thought and now she has to die.

The feel of the weight of the syringe in my pocket gives me a sense of closure, of completion. I feel my cock start to harden at the thought of her in the dress I made just for her that is currently all rolled up in a paper sack in my other hand.

Mother always told me that there was no such thing as a perfect woman but I can't believe that. She has to be out there, somewhere and until then . . . well, I'll just keep looking, keep creating perfection where none can be found.

The minute the door to my apartment shuts behind me I tumble all of the locks on the door and then lean back against the wood and breathe my first sigh of relief in over an hour.

Could it really be a cop killing these women? And if so, who? The thought of it being police officer has me shaking. Sweat beads at my hairline and rolls down my back between my shoulder blades.

I walk into the kitchen and pull a glass down from the cupboards. I fill it with water from the tap and then drink heavily as if it will clear all of the anxiety pooling deep in my gut like a poison. When my glass is empty I fill it again and drink until I need to put the glass down to catch my breath.

I close my eyes and take a deep breath before reassuring myself that I'm safe here. And I am safe. No one can get to me in my own home. Although there is a little voice in the back of my head reminding me of the snake that was left for me in a bouquet of roses. And how the killer did already get to me here.

It makes me want to jump in my car and head to Wes's house. Maybe I was wrong and there is safety in numbers. Maybe Wes and I should have stuck together all along. Was I wrong in thinking I could go it alone?

I pick up my phone to call him and realize that it's dead. I must have never plugged it in last night. Which, of course, is the first thought of anyone who drank too much Jack before going to bed. I roll my eyes at myself. What an idiot I am.

I walk into my bedroom and plug it into the charger by my bedside table before walking back into the kitchen and pulling a Chinese take-out carton from the fridge. I swear, the longer it sits in the fridge the better it is. One time, Lee's dog ate some old sushi that he threw away and puked it all up all over himself and Lee while he was sleeping on the couch next to my brother while he watched a ballgame. I was kind of pissed Liam threw it away even though it was four days old. I still would have eaten it. I did want to eat it. Shit. I'm really not a grownup after all.

I'm lost in my own thoughts of grownups and how one should probably not eat leftover sushi after, say, day three and the benefits of a well-stocked fridge and pantry that the knock at the door surprises me.

I nervously look through the peephole and relax when I see my friend. I smile as I open the door to greet them.

"Hey. What are you doing here?" I ask.

"I found something."

"What is it?" I ask eager to find out what they found. It's not until I feel the pinch in my shoulder that I realize it too late.

chapter 29

too fucking late

Wes

I NEED HER.

I need to find Claire. I hate this. I hate this fucking silent treatment. I hated watching my girl walk out of that interview room yesterday. It killed me to watch her walk away but I vowed then and there that it would be the last time she ever did it. If it's the last thing I do, I will show that woman how special she is to me, how much I love her. How much I have always loved her.

I'm not going to lie, when she walked out of that room I lost my shit. I screamed her name and begged her to come back. I did not give one fuck how many officers and detectives I knew were crammed into that observation deck, I just wanted Claire back.

Thank God for Lee.

Liam has been my best friend ever since we were born. Our families have always been close. Not too long ago I was worried how he would take the feelings I had building for his baby sister but he took it like a champ. After he TKO'd me—*total knock out*—like Muhammad Ali it was fairly smooth sailing. So, when I lost it yesterday in the interview room he dragged my ass back to his house and deposited me onto his sofa. Lee bought me a pizza and handed me a brand-new bottle of Jack that he claimed he had been saving for this very occasion. I'm still not sure how I feel about that.

This morning I woke up feeling like hammered horse shit. Most of a bottle of Jack will do that to a man. I drank a pot of coffee in Lee's kitchen before puking my guts up in the flower beds in front of his house on the way out to his car.

"Real classy, asshole," he'd grumbled before laughing as he climbed into his Tahoe and drove me back to my house so I could shower and change. When he pulled up in my driveway, the first thing we both noticed was the glaring absence of Claire's department vehicle.

"Well there's that," I had said.

"It's probably not what you think," Lee had tried to comfort me. Which, truth be told, was a little fucking awkward.

"I don't care what I think or what it looks like," I'd said. "I'm going to find her and I'm going to make it right."

"And what if she makes it difficult. What then?"

"Then I'm going to marry her ass."

After that Lee had laughed his ass off and mumbled something that sounded suspiciously like "Poor bastard."

After that I had let us into my house where Lee

made more coffee and toast in my kitchen while I showered and tried to make myself somewhat human again. I pulled on jeans and a t-shirt with my boots instead of my usual suit but I wasn't going to the office today. Today I was tracking down one wayward woman so that I could profess my love. My palms sweat and I kind of want more Jack. I'm never nervous but today I am.

At the last minute, I tuck a pancake holster into the back of my jeans—pulling my shirt out to cover it and clip my badge to my wallet and stuff both into my right back pocket just because. Lee and I were Cub Scouts way back when. I guess that *always be prepared* shit just sticks with you. I pull on my boots and grab my cell phone. I try and call Claire on my way back down the stairs to the kitchen but it just goes straight to voicemail.

"Here you go, Princess," Lee said when he handed me two pieces of toast and another cup of coffee, both of which I fell on like a starving man.

"Thank you, Cupcake," I had said before kissing his cheek. Lee swats me away and tells me to stop being an idiot before we lock up my house and climb in the car.

Now we're headed back to the station and I can't help but feel like something is wrong.

"Have you tried calling her?" I ask.

"Yeah, but it went straight to voicemail," Lee says and his brows scrunch in worry. I want to tell him that it's probably nothing but in my heart, I know that that's not true.

"Huh."

"I'm sure it's nothing," he tries to reassure me but it doesn't feel like nothing.

I was in such poor shape this morning, it's taken me almost all day just to get my shit together. The mid-afternoon sun is shining bright as we pull into the station parking lot. I look around desperately hoping to find her or spot her SUV but there's no sign of it here.

As we walk in the front door to the station, someone bumps into me in that dick way that says they did it on purpose and harder than necessary.

"Watch where you're going, asshole," someone barks. Unfortunately, I am in no mood to let it slide. Between missing Claire and the bottle of Jack I am in poor shape and spoiling for a fight.

"You got a fucking problem?" I snap.

"Yeah, you're my problem." I look up and see one of the detectives staring me down. I can't remember what his name is right now, but I'm not surprised he jumped my shit when the opportunity presented itself given the way he pants after Claire.

I smile at him letting him know that I know he has no chance in hell with Claire. "You're wasting your breath, buddy."

"We'll just see about that," he says before walking away.

"What was that all about?" Lee asks apparently having missed the whole exchange because he was conversing with the desk sergeant.

Claire's friend, Emma the ME, breezes through and Lee goes wired. Interesting. I wonder what that's all about.

"Hey Emma," I call her attention, stopping her, as

she heads for the door. "Got a minute?"

"Sure, Wes. What's up?" she asks me pointedly ignoring Liam.

"I was wondering if you've seen Claire."

"Not since lunch. I'm actually bummed she didn't tell me she was leaving. I was kind of hoping we could get dinner together. But when I looked in the conference room she was gone and half of the pages she was looking over left with her."

"Did she seem alright at lunch?" I can't help but ask.

"Yeah. She's struggling to solve this case. She wants to solve it, clear you, and do it all by the book to boot." I can't help but feel a warm glow unfurl in my chest at the thought that Claire's goals include clearing my name. She believes me.

"What was she looking over?" I ask.

"Oh, just the autopsy reports and personal lists from the crimes scenes."

"Why?" Lee asks.

"Because if it's not Wes connected to all three murders then it had to be someone and the best bet would be someone from this station," she explains.

"That's crazy!" Liam shouts clearly angry that she would point a finger at one of his officers, but I can't help feeling like there's a frisson of truth in there somewhere.

I take off for the conference room and see that papers are scattered all over the table haphazardly and the chair that she was obviously sitting in has been swung back quickly—then not tucked back into the table as if she left in a hurry.

The hairs on the back of my neck stand on end.

I pick up several of the papers from the table and study them. Emma was right, it's a hodgepodge of the autopsy reports on all three victims with Claire's notes made in the margins. Then there it is, sitting right in the middle of the table. A list of names with check marks next to them. Claire was doing just as Emma said she had been. She was looking to see who was at each and every crime scene.

Suddenly looking at the list one name stands out and it's like a punch to the gut. I need to get to Claire. *Now*. My only hope is that I'm not too fucking late.

I race back through to the lobby where Liam is quietly arguing with Emma but there is no doubt in my mind that they are arguing. I snap my fingers in front of his face.

"We gotta go, man."

"Give me a minute," he says. "I'm in the middle of something."

"No time. We gotta go now." He must hear something in my voice because all of a sudden he's barking commands at me as we race back out the door.

"What's going on?" he clips out as we run for his truck.

"We have to get to Claire," I shout. "There's no time. I know who it is."

As we race back through town towards Claire's apartment, I have never been more glad that Lee drives like a bat out of hell. He pulls into the parking lot and I jump out of the SUV before he's even come to a complete stop. In my gut I know that there is no time.

I race up the steps to her door, pushing myself to

go faster and faster. I knock on the door and call out her name.

"Claire, it's Wes. Are you home, honey?"

But no one answers. It's complete and total silence until I hear her scream. I reach behind me for my gun as I place my boot to the door and kick it open. I hear Lee climbing the stairs behind me but when the door swings fully open and I see her lying there in that creepy fucking dress with that asshole's hands wrapped around her neck and the blank look on her face—I realize I was too fucking late.

So, I do the only thing my brain will let me. I raise my gun and pull the trigger.

chapter 30

fade to black

Claire

I DON'T WAKE UP with a start, but in stages. Ironic for all the times I have been cast into consciousness with a quickness after a night terror only to wake up and realize I am safe and fine. Now, my brain finally lets me ease into being awake and I find myself in a real-life nightmare.

I feel my body pitch back and forth like a ship tossed about on the sea. One time, when I was nine, I was sure that I could man the two-man sailboat that Lee and Wes were racing that summer before they left for boot camp. *Anything you can do, I can do better and all that.*

But there were life lessons to be had here—like beware of snakes and slashed tires and men who come on too strong but I wasn't listening. I never listen.

We'd had a summer storm come up suddenly. Having never actually been taught how to sail, I had no idea that I needed to check the weather before I took a boat out. And by take a boat out, I mean, I stole their boat.

One would think that by now I would have learned my lesson, but no, I'm hard headed like that.

Back then I was minding my own business toodle-ing around when a huge gust of wind caught my sail and pitched my little boat to one side, spinning it around, and then back to the other side again. I was flopped around like a shopping bag caught in a breeze. Where you run and run after it, feeling guilty that you'll never catch it, but no matter how hard you try because no one likes a litterer, you can't catch it. That's exactly what it was like. And that's exactly how my body feels right now as my body is pulled and twisted and flopped about rather unceremoniously.

I test my toes—wiggling them as if my life depends on it, because it likely does—and nada, bupkis. Shit, shit, shit! I try my hands, my fingers, something anything. The only thing I seem to be able to move is my right eyelid, my left is paralyzed like the rest of my body.

Paralyzed.

Panic seized me and robs me of the breath from my lungs as I realize I have absolutely no way to protect myself. Just like Bonnie, Tammy, and Tawnya, I'm going to die.

My body is rolled backwards and I am flopped on my back. I feel my one moveable eye go wide as I recognize the man looming over me is none other than Detective Abraham Cruz. The man who has been cognizant of my feelings for weeks and acted as if he was truly protective of me, worried about me. He asked me out several times pretending to be interested in me when all along he was ruthlessly planning my murder.

He smiles a blinding white smile at me that crinkles the corners of his eyes. I can't believe I thought him handsome. I can't believe that in the midst of my relationship turmoil with Wes, I thought I might regret turning down this kind, handsome man who was clearly interested in me. The thought makes my stomach roil.

"I'm glad you're awake," he says as he straddles my thighs, pinning them down. "Do you like your dress? I made this one special for you."

I begin to blink my one eye furiously. It feels like it rolls around in my head like a marble but I'm still able to take stock of my dress—a word I would never like to hear again if I survive this, which likely, I won't.

The dress is made of light pink fabric with tiny, little rosebuds all over it in a slightly darker shade of pink. There are delicate lace cuffs at my wrists and a Peter Pan collar at my collar bone made of the same material.

My first thought is that I look like I escaped from the Juniper Creek compound on *Big Love*, my second is that I am surely going to die.

"I knew you'd like it," Cruz says as he pushes the voluminous skirt ever so slowly up my legs.

His eyes glitter at me with lust and I know to him that this is a seduction. Not too long ago, Wes looked at me the same way before he crawled over my body in his big bed and made love to me. I let my eye close on the sweet memory. I want that to be the last thing I see before I die.

"Why?" I ask but my lack of muscle control makes it come out more of a *Unghiiiiigh.* Fortunately for me he's feeling like talking.

"I thought you were perfect." He sighs as if the world weighs heavy on his shoulders. "But you were such a disappointment. At least, we'll be able to enjoy each other this one time before I move on."

I watch with a weird sense of detachment as his hands caress my newly exposed thighs.

"No!" I scream but it comes out *Nurrr* through my closed lips.

"Don't worry," he reassures me. "I'll find my perfection in a new town. I'm truly sorry it wasn't you."

There's a knock at the door. Cruz puts his hand over my mouth to silence me.

"Claire, it's Wes. Are you home, honey?" Wes calls through the thin slab of fake wood. Cruz holds a finger up to his lips to emphasize his orders to be quiet.

But fuck that.

After a moment of silence passes, he reaches for his belt buckle and I know this is it. I'm beginning to really panic. It can't end like this. It can't all be for nothing. I scream at the top of my lungs, pushing the noise as hard and as fast as I can out of my body and hoping it reaches Wes before it's too late and he leaves.

"I was hoping we could enjoy each other first," Cruz growls at me. "But it appears you'll have to die first. Don't worry at all, my pet. I'll still enjoy you after."

Acid burns in my stomach at the thought of him touching me after I'm dead. He wraps his hands around my neck and begins to squeeze. He applies light pressure at first. He's testing the waters—enjoying his kill.

Then gradually, he squeezes my neck a little harder. It becomes increasingly harder to breathe. Black spots dance in front of my eyes and I realize it's too late. Wes didn't hear me after all. It's all over now, or it will be in another minute or two. And a calmness, a sense of peace washes over me.

I love you, Wes.

The words dance around in my mind as if I can send them out into the universe and somehow, when I'm gone, he'll know that I have always loved him. Maybe he can find a peace in that too.

And then the door explodes, splintering everywhere as Wes kicks the door in and my brother, Liam follows him in. He raises his sig. I always thought it was kind of funny that Wes was so set in his ways that after years of trotting around the globe doing God knows what, God knows where as a SEAL with a Sig Sauer P226 he still fancies them. Old habits never die and all that.

And then he pulls the trigger.

I wish I could stick around and enjoy the show. Wes's face is fierce with fire and determination. He's a warrior through and through and it's a sight to behold. But then everything fades to black.

epilogue

perfect

Three weeks later . . .

THIS MORNING I RECEIVED three dozen daisies and a note.

Meet me at the house at 4 PM. Come around the back to the patio.
I love you always,
Wes

My heart had thumped in my chest and I bit my lip and smiled at my flower delivery men. After the rattlesnake in the roses, flowers had lost their appeal. I wouldn't have trusted just anyone to bring me flowers and Wes knew that so these were delivered by my dad. My Wes has an eye for detail. He's also cognizant of my needs and wants—of which there have been more than usual after my attack.

"He's a good man, baby," he had said to me.

"I know," I had whispered back.

"Be happy," Dad said softly.

"I am."

After my dad left my apartment, I climbed in the shower. My body is still sore from being tossed around like a rag doll by Cruz so I let the hot water beat down on my body for a bit before I scrub every inch.

I turn off the taps and dry off with a towel before heading into my closet where I pull on panties and a matching bra. Wes and I haven't been intimate since my attack but I'm hoping to change that tonight so I choose a delicate lavender silk pair with care. I don't want to look like I'm trying too hard and I'm still battered and bruised so I cover my lace with black leggings and a vee-neck t-shirt.

I twist my towel dried hair up into a messy bun on top of my head and slide my favorite chucks onto my feet. I pull on a denim jacket and slip my car keys and phone into the pockets.

I walk out of my apartment, locking the door behind me and head down the stairs to my car. I have no idea what Wes has planned for tonight and I don't care. I just want to be with him.

A happy calm, a contentment rolls over me as I drive across town to the neighborhood we all grew up in. The one that Wes still lives in to this day. I park my car in the driveway and follow his instructions to come around back—bypassing the front door for the old wooden gate with lattice trim at the top.

I pull the string to pop the latch and walk right into a secret garden fitting of one of my favorite childhood novels. Mom and I read that book over and over again. We both loved it and couldn't get enough. I used to vow one day I would live in a house with a secret garden and Wes would be my husband.

Silly childhood thoughts bounce around in my brain as I take in the yards and yards of twinkle fairy lights that sparkle in the trees and dozens of brightly colored paper lanterns that hang from the wood and lattice pergola that covers the patio. Tons of candles glow and flicker in the cool spring breeze on the black iron and glass table in the center while music plays softly.

And there are daisies and violets everywhere. And not one rose.

I look to Wes who stands in the middle of it all in jeans and a blue button-down shirt tucked in at his trim waist with a worn, brown leather belt with a silver buckle. He has the sleeves rolled up to show his corded forearms and his feet are bare.

I suddenly feel self-conscious looking at all of the beauty that is Wes standing before me. I feel my face heat with a blush that I'm sure is covering more than my cheeks. I duck my head as I brush loose tendrils of hair back behind my ear.

"Look at me, Claire," he says, his voice sure and true. I look up at him and what I see there catches my breath in my chest. "You're perfect."

"Wh-what," I have to stop and clear my throat. My voice is unsteady or shaky at best after being strangled. "What's all this?"

"Dance with me?" he asks and the tentative smile that plays on his mouth makes him look more like the boy that I knew and less like a thirty-eight-year-old man. I can't help but accept.

"Okay," I rasp. I kick off my shoes as he makes his way down the steps from the deck to me and meet him in the middle of the lawn.

"May I take your jacket?" he asks me and I bite my lip and nod as he slides the denim down my shoulders and places it on an iron bench near where we're standing.

Wes returns to me and wraps his arm around me and I place my hand at the back of his neck. Wes smiles down at me before he takes my hand in his and holds it out to our sides as he slowly begins to sway and circle us to the music. It suddenly dawns on me that I have never danced with Wes before. And he's really good at it.

I can't help but sigh and it's frustrated at best.

"What is it, baby?" he asks me, his voice gruff with emotion.

"When will you ever stop saving me, Wes?"

"Never, honey. I'll always catch you when you fall."

I hate that my voice sounds small and unsure when the word slips out from my lips but it does. "Forever?"

"Until the day I die." Wes's voice rings true and strong.

I look over his shoulder as we continue to move to the music. We silently dance to the quiet music for awhile, until Wes breaks that silence by rocking my world.

"You have to know, Claire."

"Know what?" I ask.

"That I am hopelessly and irrevocably in love with you," he says as he stops our swaying. My throat catches and his hands rise up slowly to cup my cheeks. He holds my face tenderly in his hands as he looks into my eyes with so much love and light that I just want to sink into it. "Marry me, Claire."

"Do you think it's too soon?" I ask feeling a little unsure, not of us or of Wes but of me. "We've only been together for a little while."

"I have loved you forever, Claire."

"You can't mean—" I start but he interrupts me gently.

"You have been mine for forever, Claire, and I have been yours. No matter what's happened or what will happen. None of it matters because I have loved you one way or another since the day you were born. It's grown and it's changed over the years and I know that it will continue to grow because we will tend it and nurture it for the rest of our lives."

"But—" I start and he interrupts me again.

"Whatever it is we'll get through it, Claire. It's not you against me or me against you anymore. I promise you that it is us together and we can take on anything." I feel tears prick my eyes. For the first time in a long time they're happy ones. "Say it," he says softly.

"Yes."

"You're going to marry me?" he asks.

"Yes, Wes," I say through the huge smile that splits my face and the sweet tears rolling down my face. "I'll marry you."

His mouth crushes down on mine hard and fast before he scoops me up into his arms and twirls me around. I throw my head back and laugh.

Wes places me back on my feet before letting me go. He reaches into his pants pocket and produces a small velvet box before dropping down on one knee.

"Give me your hand, baby." And probably for the first time ever in history, I do what he asks me to and hold out my hand.

He opens the box and the biggest diamond I have ever seen glitters on the satin pillow. Wes plucks it up and tosses the box over his shoulder to the grass before sliding the ring up past my knuckle.

A perfect fit. Just like Wes and me.

I sit down on his knee and wrap my arms around his neck. I touch my lips to his before smiling. "Could you have found a bigger ring?" I laugh.

"Nope," he says against my mouth. "I want it to be seen from space. I told you I was done fucking around, baby. You're mine now." His whiskey eyes burn bright into mine.

"Now and forever."

"Abso-fucking-lutely," he says.

We tumble down into the grass all hands and mouths and bodies. It's soft and sweet and a little wild, just like Wes. And then he makes love to me as the sun sets in the middle of our own little secret garden. I guess some childhood dreams really do come true.

And it was perfect.

the end . . . for now

playlist

This Is How a Heart Breaks—Rob Thomas
Ain't No Other Man—Christina Aguilera
Better Man—Little Big Town
How's It Going To Be—Third Eye Blind
Bad At Love—Halsey
Bad Blood—Taylor Swift
Bleeding Love—Leona Lewis
Come Over—Sam Hunt
Love Me Harder—Ariana Grande and The Weeknd
Every Breath You Take—The Police
I Know Places—Taylor Swift
Face Down—Red Jumpsuit Apparatus
Perfect—Ed Sheeran

about jennifer rebecca

Jennifer is a thirty something lover of words, all words: the written, the spoken, the sung (even poorly), the sweet, the funny, and even the four letter variety. She is a native of San Diego, California where she grew up reading the Brownings and Rebecca with her mother and Clifford and the Dog who Glowed in the Dark with her dad, much to her mother's dismay.

Jennifer is a graduate of California State University San Marcos where she studied Criminology and Justice Studies. She is also a member of Alpha Xi Delta.

10 years ago, she was swept off her feet by her very own sailor. Today, they are happily married and the parents of a 9 year old and 7 year old twins. She lives in East Texas where she can often be found on the soccer fields, drawing with her children, or reading. Jennifer is convinced that if she puts her fitbit on one of the dogs, she might finally make her step goals. She loves a great romance, an alpha hero, and lots and lots of laughter.

stalk her

Website
JenniferRebeccaAuthor.com

Newsletter
JenniferRebeccaAuthor.com/Newsletter

Facebook
facebook.com/JenniferRebeccaAuthor

Twitter
@JenniRLreads

Instagram
@JenniRLreads

BookBub
bookbub.com/authors/jennifer-rebecca

Book+Main
bookandmainbites.com/users/22594

Dangerous Dames Facebook Group
facebook.com/groups/JRDangerousDames

also by jennifer rebecca

The Funerals and Obituaries Mysteries
Dead and Buried
Dead and Gone, Coming Summer 2018

The Murder on Ice Mysteries
Attack Zone
Layback, Coming 2019

The Southern Heartbeats Series
Stand (Vol. 1)
Joy (a Southern Heartbeat Holiday), previously featured in then Love, Snow, & Mistletoe Anthology for St. Jude
Whiskey Lullabye (Vol. 2)
Mercy (a Southern Heartbeats Short), free on Wattpad
Just a Dream (Vol. 3), Coming Soon

The Claire Goodnite Thrillers
Tell Me A Story
Tuck Me In Tight
Say A Sweet Prayer
Kiss Me Goodnight

The Wanted Kindle World
Church Bells

VOLUME 3 OF THE *claire goodnite* SERIES

say a/sweet prayer

Sneak Peek

Subject to change

raw

Pain.

What a stupid little word to describe what I am feeling right now. Such a mundane word to explain the white-hot lightning rips through my torso in the vicinity of where my heart used to be. It sears so acutely that my breath catches in my throat.

"No!" someone screams. I think it was me.

Hands grab me from behind to stop me from closing the gap between the bloody body on the altar of my family church. These slabs of muscle and bone and joint and tendons restrain me, holding me back from the jarring loss, the cold truth of what has come to pass.

"Let me go!"

"No," someone says. I don't know who. I don't care either. I can't stop staring at the broken remains of someone I loved above all else. Someone who managed to do the unthinkable, to break down my walls and invade my heart.

Before I had looked at victims and thought why couldn't I save them? Or it should have been me. But looking at the shell of what had been as it's splayed on the plush carpet of the altar steps I know without a doubt that I would trade places in a heartbeat. If only it was my blood that was spilled and not theirs.

Greif.

If this is what grief feels like I don't want it. I want

to go back to this morning when my life was normal, I had the world at my feet, and my family was whole. I feel raw. Exposed. I'm a wound that's been flayed open.

Maybe this is shock. I don't know. All I do know is that the world is a darker place tonight. This is not a loss that I or anyone else will get over. Not now. Not ever. My name is Detective Claire Goodnite and everything has changed.

I guess it's best we say our prayers . . .

Get release alerts by signed up for Jennifer Rebecca's newsletter

www.jenniferrebeccaauthor.com/newsletter

* 9 7 8 1 7 3 2 0 7 4 7 2 9 *